LOVE BY CHANCE

Blake Allwood

Blake Allwood
Visit my website at www.blakeallwood.com

Printed in the United States of America
Box Elder, SD

First Printing: June 2020
Second Printing: October 2021

ISBN: 978-1-956727-09-8

Library of Congress Control Number: 2021920118

Titles by Blake Allwood:
<u>Transitions Series</u>
Aiden Inspired
Suzie Empowered
Bobby Transformed

<u>By Chance Series</u>
Love By Chance (1)
Another Chance With Love (2)
Taking A Chance For Love (3)

<u>Big Bend Series</u>
Love's Legacy (1)
Love's Heirloom (2)
Love's Bequest (3)

<u>Romantic Series</u>
Romantic Renovations (1)
Romantic Rescue (2)
Romantic Recon (coming soon)

<u>Coming Home Series</u>
Tenacious

Purchase at:
https://readerlinks.com/mybooks/4515

Join Blake's email list to get advance notice of new
books
and receive his occasional newsletter:
https://www.blakeallwood.com

Thank you to the following people for their assistance:

Kristopher Miller – Developmental Editor
Aryl Shanti – Copy Editor
Jo Bird – Line Editor
Janine Cloud – Proofreader

Version Two
Renee Mizar - Proofreader

A special thank you goes to all my friends and family who supported me, I couldn't have done it without you.

And finally, an extra special thanks to my Husband who continues to tolerate me no matter how many of these rabbit holes I keep going down (and I seem to keep going down them).

Two Years Earlier: Martin

Peter was always acting silly, so I didn't pay much attention when he crawled in front of me, blocking my view of the TV. We'd just gotten back from visiting his horrible mother and were cuddling in front of an old Christmas movie.

"Martin, I've loved you since we first met. I don't want to spend one more night without you being mine. Would you do me the honor of being my husband?"

I stared at him for what must have seemed like ages because it appeared he was about to start panicking, as if he expected me to say no.

"Martin?" he finally prompted.

I stared at the ring and caught my breath. "Peter? You're serious? You want to marry me?"

Peter smiled, a tear leaking from his eye. "More than anything in the world, I want you to be my husband, Martin."

I drew in a deep breath. Was I ready at twenty-three to marry a man I'd met less than a year ago? I was overcome with how much he meant to me. "He makes me happy every day, he's my best friend, and he gives a really good blowjob." I only realized I'd been talking out loud when I saw Peter smile.

"I do give a good blowjob," he said. "So, what do you say, wanna put claims on this mouth... so it belongs only to you?"

"Oh, hell yeah! I really do," I said and threw myself into his arms.

The next morning, we rushed to my parents' home to make the announcement. Both my parents pulled Peter into a bear hug, welcoming him to our family. I was so proud of them. They were conservative Texans, but their love for me overcame everything else. They were the definition of good people.

Unfortunately, it didn't go so well with Peter's mom. I referred to her as Matilda the Hun because the woman was the epitome of hate. No, not against gay people, she *loved* them and would drone on and on for hours about her involvement with PFLAG. No, she didn't hate *gay* people, she hated *me*.

We didn't get the chance to tell her until a week before Christmas. She'd been suffering from intense migraines that kept her locked in her room with the lights out for days on end. She refused to go to the doctor because, according to the beast, "That's what ridiculous people who don't have anything better to do with their time or money do."

His mom was still struggling with a headache when Peter decided we couldn't put it off any longer. We stopped by her house one evening to announce our news. She smiled, but I could tell she wasn't happy.

She managed to kiss Peter and congratulate him, but when she kissed my cheek, she whispered, "We'll see about this," then leaned back and smiled like she hadn't just threatened me.

I just shook my head. I'd had enough of Matilda the Hun. If she wasn't happy for us, then so be it.

When I told Peter what she'd said, he laughed it off, as usual, dismissing it as "...just her way. The headache probably just made it sound harsher than she meant it to be."

Despite what Peter said, our engagement did nothing but raise the heat in that particular oven.

What had previously been abuse, which had been bad enough, shifted to being downright evil.

Christmas Eve had been Peter's family day. He'd explained to me that his family usually celebrated on Christmas Eve, then they'd spend Christmas Day with Matilda's sisters. I'd agreed to spend Christmas Eve with him at Matilda's house, then we'd spend Christmas Day with my family. That night, well, let's just say it was one for the history books.

Matilda was clearly on the warpath from the minute we walked in. Throughout the evening, when Peter was around, she'd smile and say how nice it was that he'd found true love, but when she got me alone, she slammed into me with well-rehearsed venom.

As things escalated, it took everything in me not to just walk out, but I was so surprised by the new level of hate, I wasn't able to get my wits about me in time to stand up for myself.

By the time the evening ended, the witch had called me every name she could think of. I'd been called a whore, slut, social climber, and an asswipe.

The most memorable moment was while I was warming up a casserole I'd brought. She snuck up behind me and said that if she'd been a man, she would've beaten my ass in the street.

Finally, I'd had enough. I was going to have to leave or, at least, get away from her. I sat in a chair in the living room, pretending to watch a football game. Luckily, other guests were in there, and the bitch couldn't get me alone, which saved me from any more of her verbal abuse.

After we left, Peter was obviously upset I had disappeared. He laid into me for leaving the table and not helping with cleanup.

"Peter," I replied, "did you not hear all the crap your mother said to me tonight?"

He turned his gaze on me momentarily as he drove us home. "What do you mean?" he asked.

"Peter, your mother pulled out all the stops. I've *never* been insulted like that before. She even told me I smell like ass."

Peter laughed. "No, that's just her odd sense of humor."

"No, this was not her sense of humor, Peter. This was a series of vicious attacks against me. The fact that she did it so you couldn't hear means she didn't want you to know. That isn't humor. That's deliberate hatred."

Peter immediately became defensive. "My mother doesn't hate anyone. She's the most supportive woman I know."

"Yeah, *to you*, she is, but not to me." As the conversation went on, and I told Peter more and more of what Matilda had said, he became angrier, but not at his mother. He grew angrier with me.

When we arrived home, Peter marched straight into the house. As I walked in behind him, he turned to me with the same derision I'd seen in his mother's face earlier that night. "I won't be forced to choose between my mother, a loving and caring woman who'd do anything for me, and you, who clearly has some strange agenda going on."

It was impossible to describe how, at that moment, all hope, happiness and joy that I'd associated with loving Peter Reed began to crumble. I stared at his face, which expressed all the bias I had heard in his words. I wanted to scream at him, tell him that if he loved me, he wouldn't let his mother win this stupid war she was waging against me. Instead, I saw Peter for what he really was. He was not someone who would love me unconditionally. He was not the man I'd agreed to marry.

As my broken-hearted tears cascaded down my face, I stared at the man I was engaged to. "I love you, Peter, with all my heart, but I won't allow you, your mother, or anyone for that matter, to treat me this way."

Peter, still angry, replied, "Thankfully, I got to see you for what you are *before* we got married."

The comment crushed what little hope I had left. I gathered a few of my things, got into my car, and drove to my parent's house.

Managing to call my parents on my way to let them know I was coming, I was met at the door by my ever-solid father and mother. They both held me while I cried.

We sat in the fancy living room they'd decorated for Christmas, and I told them everything. Although it was clear my parents were shocked, they didn't question me, and when I was done, they both hugged me again.

"I will not be insulted and ridiculed," I said at last.

My mother kissed me on the forehead. "No, honey. You were taught that you are valuable and worthwhile. You were taught to love yourself."

"I loved him, too," I said, and then cried even more. After the final bout of tears had fallen, I stood up and kissed my dad and mom on the cheek. "I think he was right. It is better that we found this out before we got married." Then, twisting the engagement ring off my finger, I went up to my old bedroom, leaving my parents downstairs.

As I lay in my childhood bed, I thought about all that had happened, how much I'd loved Peter, and how much I was going to miss him. By the time I finally drifted to sleep, I had assured myself I'd rather be alone than with someone who wouldn't stand up for me. I hadn't offended his mother or put her in a situation where she felt uncomfortable. That's what she'd done to me, and instead of Peter standing up and holding his mother accountable, he'd taken her side. I'd never be able to forgive him for that, even if he showed up and begged me to.

The next morning, I got up early. I knew Peter planned to go to a friends' house to see their kids unwrap presents from Santa. I drove to the apartment we rented together, packed up as many of my belongings as I could, and piled them into my old Subaru.

I left a note that simply read, *You were right. It is best to know now.* I left my key, as well as the engagement ring, on the table next to the letter.

I knew I'd always remember Peter as my first love, but that wasn't enough. I needed my spouse to support me. As I drove, the pain became so intense I had to stop several times on the way back to my parents' house and take deep breaths to compose myself. When I got back, however, something had shifted inside me. A spark of life had reignited in my core, a spark that indicated I'd survive this.

At the end of the day, I'd been confronted with a vicious and unfounded hatred. And I'd chosen to stand up for myself. I vowed that from that day forward, I'd never allow anyone to speak to me the way Matilda the Hun had. I'd be my own champion. I'd never again expect a man to be that for me.

***

It was all hands on deck the week after Christmas. My best friend Janice all but moved in with my parents as I processed being single again. Even my sister Trish was uncharacteristically nice to me as I wallowed in self-pity.

Janice eventually forced me out on the town for New Year's Eve. We already had plans to attend a ball being held by the newspaper I wrote restaurant reviews for.

"I'm taking him out," she announced to everyone in the house, pointing her finger at me when I moaned. "And you are gonna like it!"

My mother was zero help and just giggled as she walked away.

"Janice, I'm really not into it," I whined.

"That's because you've become a hermit, and enough is enough," she proclaimed.

I didn't have the energy to argue with her. Besides, I did want to get out again. I was sick of feeling sorry for myself.

"Okay, but I'm driving myself. If I don't feel like staying until the clock strikes twelve, then I want to be able to leave without ruining your night."

Janice glared at me like she was going to argue but thought better of it. "Okay, deal. Now, let's go get ready. I can't wait to show you off as the city's newest, most eligible bachelor."

I groaned as she pushed me up the stairs.

I was shocked at how much better I felt being out of the house. My heart still felt like it was broken into several pieces, but the fact I wasn't sitting in my parents' house moping was a definite improvement.

The party was a hoot, and it made me happy to see my coworkers laughing and cutting-up with one another.

Around nine, my boss, Elizabeth, introduced me to her college roommate, Kristine Diaz, who'd come in from Fort Lauderdale for a visit. She and I began talking, and when she heard what I did for a living, she laughed. "Elizabeth has sent me some of your work to read. You're funny and respectful of the restaurants at the same time. Have you ever considered a move to South Florida?" she asked.

I looked at her blankly. "I haven't really, no. I grew up in Texas, I've never considered moving anywhere else."

Kristine was drunk but smiled at me and gave me her card. I looked down at it. *Kristine Diaz. Assignment Editor, Fort Lauderdale Press.* "If you change your mind, all you need to do is email me," she said before she drifted away into the crowd.

I honestly didn't think much about it, especially when 11:30 came and went, and I realized I was still at the party. I'd barely thought about Peter—okay, so that was probably a lie, but I hadn't thought about him as much as I had the previous week. Midnight came, and Janice gave me a huge kiss right on the smacker, giggling when I made gagging noises.

"You are the worst straight man in the world, Martin Williams," she said with a flourish.

"Um, I'm not a straight man, *chica*. You need to get your gaydar fixed again!"

This was an ongoing joke between us, and she pulled me into a warm hug. "I'm so glad you came. It feels good to see you back on your feet. Even if you are a little wobbly."

I smiled at her and hugged her back. "You're the best friend on the planet, even if you are evil."

Janice chuckled. She knew she was a handful and made no apologies for it.

By the time January third came, I found myself more than a little intrigued by the idea of moving to a different town. Yeah, it was kind of like running away, but I knew that and was comfortable with it. I'd followed up Kristine's suggestion and looked up the paper in Fort Lauderdale. It was large enough to have a department with more than one restaurant critic.

There was—for real—an ad in the paper seeking another critic full-time, with a salary almost double what I made here in Austin. All that aside, the thought of a fresh start felt right, or as right as anything could at the moment.

I sent Kristine an email along with my resume, telling her that if she was serious about the offer, I'd be interested in an interview.

She called me literally ten minutes after I clicked send.

"Martin. Hi, this is Kristine Diaz with the *Fort Lauderdale Press*. Are you free now?" she asked as soon as I'd said hello.

I chuckled. "I can be, maybe in a couple of hours."

"Oh, my plane leaves in three hours. Can you meet me at the airport?" she asked.

"Sure, say, in an hour?" I asked, surprised at the speed of it all.

"Perfect," she replied. "I'll text you where I'm at. I can get checked in, then I'll meet you at one of the restaurants outside the security gate."

I rushed to get ready and made it to Austin Airport with just enough time to park and get to the restaurant. I detested being late, especially to an interview.

Kristine was waiting for me when I arrived.

"Hello, Mrs. Diaz," I said, trying to sound professional.

She chuckled. "Oh, honey, I was drunk off my ass at the party when I last spoke to you. You can just call me Kristine."

I nodded and smiled.

"I've looked over some of your work since the party, and it's impressive. I especially like your critiques. They are the right blend of wit and professionalism. That's important in our region."

I nodded again. "Is the position doing only restaurant critiques?"

She smiled. "Yes, this is a full-time restaurant critic position. It's a lot of work, though, not like what you've done here in Austin. You'll be given an area of the city. Your job will be to visit each restaurant and put a critique on our site for each one. It's something new we're doing this year. We want to combine the paper and our presence online and ensure we give Google and TripAdvisor a bit of *local* competition."

"Sounds like my dream job," I admitted. "When would you want me to start?"

She laughed again. "Are you that confident I'm going to offer you the job then?"

I smiled. "No, not confident, just hopeful."

"Yes, I'd love to hire you, if you are willing to move to Florida. And I'd like you to start as soon as possible. How about February first?" she asked with a smile.

I thought for a moment before I returned eye contact. "I guess it's lucky that I just got out of a very nasty breakup with my ex-fiancé. *He* dumped me Christmas Eve." I deliberately emphasized the he part. We were still in the South, and I wanted to be out of the closet *before* I made a huge life change.

"Well, *he*"—she emphasized the word—"sounds like a total idiot. What man in his right mind would dump a catch like you?"

"An idiot for sure. Let's go with that."

She laughed, then glanced at her watch. "So, what's it going to be? Wanna throw caution to the wind and come work for me?"

"Sure, it sounds like exactly what I need right now. But I'll need a place to live."

"Not a problem. We have a corporate rental that just became empty. The rent's paid up until March. You can either take the lease yourself, or I can help you find someplace else. The best part is the apartment is just a couple blocks from the paper, so you'll be close by while getting your bearings."

Just then, they called for her plane. "Oh, crap! I still have to go through security. I'm so excited, Martin," she said as she grabbed her carry-on bag and scurried toward security check-in. "I'll call you tomorrow to set up all the details, okay?" she asked, not waiting for an answer as she disappeared around the corner.

I waved at her retreating form. Had I actually just taken a job in Fort Lauderdale? What was my family going to say? What the heck was Janice going to say? Would Peter notice or even care?

No, scrap that last thought. It didn't matter if he cared or not. I was setting myself up for a new and much-improved life. Peter was not going to be a part of that.

***

When I gave my two weeks' notice, my boss told me she was going to go commit violent acts against her friend for stealing me away from her. Then she admitted she sort of set it up.

"You're wasting your talent here at such a small paper. We'll miss you but I think it's the right move for your professional development and on a personal note, I'm really proud of you for taking the opportunity." At that, I had to swallow the lump in my throat. I was touched actually that she'd put me before the requirements of the paper.

My parents were beside themselves with concern. "You're too vulnerable right now to make this kind of decision," my mother moaned.

I hugged her. "Mom, I love you so much, but even you've said some of the best decisions we make are during life's ups and downs."

My sister, Trish, acted like she was glad I was going to be out of her hair, but I could tell she was feeling bad about me leaving. All in all, everything about pulling up stakes was pretty easy, except for leaving my family and best friend.

Janice took me out on the town for a final hoorah, and we both got drunk and cried on each other's shoulders. It was emotional healing at its best. "You'll come visit me when you need sunshine and beachfront," I kept telling her. She'd high-five me every time and say, "Damn straight."

I shipped the few belongings I needed or wanted to the new office. I looked around my family home, knowing I wouldn't be able to come back without a long drive or flight, which felt strange and gave me a heavy heart. At the same time, a sense of nervous excitement filled me, realizing what a big moment this new start was for me.

I went out to eat that morning at my favorite brunch restaurant, although I admit, I did make sure Peter wasn't there before I went inside.

I'd decided to go to the airport alone. I needed to do this by myself so I could say goodbye to my hometown of Austin. It was also a goodbye to all the pain I'd felt over the breakup with Peter.

Despite having to have my seat upright, I adjusted myself to be as comfortable as possible, while the plane prepared for takeoff. I felt a sense of relief about moving on with my future. I thought to myself with a smile, *goodbye old life and hello new.*

Present Day: Martin

When we arrived in the conference room, the attorney was waiting for us. Kristine and I walked in feeling cool and confident.

The meeting was between the newspaper's attorney and a disgruntled restaurant and brewery owner who'd gotten a negative review because, well to put it mildly, his restaurant's service sucked.

When I told Janice, she sent me a GIF with three sassy gay guys walking into a bar. They'd stop and pose before sashaying into the room over and over again. I showed Kristine, and before we left the office, we practiced walking into the meeting with that as our guide. It was a great morale booster to know she was fast becoming a friend as well as being my boss.

Upon seeing the attorney, Kristine immediately introduced us. "Chris, this is Martin, the one who wrote the review. Martin, our attorney Chris. So, what's the prognosis?" Kristine asked.

The attorney sighed. "You've been with the paper for two years now, and you've not had anyone come after you before. That being said, your review was tough on them, but it wasn't horrible. As long as you can justify it, even if it goes to court, you should be fine."

"It's so frustrating. I wrote that review in such a way that if the restaurant owners and management wanted, they could improve, and I'd be able to visit again at a future date. Do they know that Kristine was with me for the review?" I asked.

"No," the attorney said, "and we need to keep that just between us for now. If we can't resolve this here, that information may be useful in the future."

When we'd first gotten word that we were being sued for the review, Chris had warned Kristine that this particular owner was well known for playing games to discredit reviewers. A similar incident had occurred a year or so ago.

When the door opened, a short and pudgy red-faced man, who was introduced by Chris as Mr. Peady, the owner, came in with his attorney. A few moments later, another man, this one significantly more attractive, came in behind them.

"Hi, I'm Elian Whitman, I'm part owner of the restaurant" he said deliberately looking us in the eye as he shook our hands.

The men were followed by a woman who appeared to be in her early sixties and introduced herself as the moderator. When both attorneys indicated they were ready to begin, we launched right in.

"This is a situation where a young upstart just wants to get his name in print, and we won't have it," the obviously passionate owner declared. "He can't be allowed to build his name by damaging our restaurant's stellar reputation. These lies will not be tolerated!" As he said that last part, he banged his hand on the table to emphasize his words and stared me directly in the face.

Kristine and I glanced at each other. Even though we'd anticipated this, the speech was ridiculous and although we were determined to remain professional, it was hard to sit here and not roll our eyes. The owner's partner, Elian, seemed to be watching us closely throughout the proceedings. It was my guess his job was to read the environment, then help his partner with any observations. It continued to get more difficult to keep my feelings hidden as the irate man spouted off. To be honest, I'd never been good at schooling my emotions anyway. I knew this guy, Elian, could probably read me like a book.

When the red-faced man finished his tirade, Elian asked if the moderator would allow the attorneys and our party a chance to talk before we continued.

The moderator hesitated before speaking. "That is something that should have already been done prior to the meeting."

"Yes," Elian agreed. "I understand, but I just got back into town and haven't been available before now."

The mediator shook her head and stood to leave. "You have fifteen minutes, then I'll return. And we *will* either continue, or this mediation will be concluded. Understood?"

Elian nodded.

As soon as she left, Elian turned toward his partner. "Did you speak to our employees about the review?"

The owner must've felt trapped because his already red face deepened to a shade of purple. He responded with a huff, "Of course I did."

"What did they say?" Elian asked.

"They said it was a lie. They didn't even remember who he was."

Elian then turned to me. "Can you tell me exactly what you experienced?"

Both attorneys tried to stop the dialogue with little success. Elian turned to his representative. "It is the responsibility of all of us to resolve this dispute in an equitable way." He then turned to our attorney. "If I'm comfortable with the reviewer's explanation, I'll be willing to drop the lawsuit."

His co-owner sputtered, and seemed like he might explode right in front of us. When he tried to speak, however, the younger man put his hand up to stop him. Turning to me, he asked again, "Will you explain exactly what you found when you visited the restaurant?"

"The review pretty much explained it," I answered honestly, "but I'd be happy to go back over the details." I'd learned long ago to document events well, especially if my reviews reflected negatively. I opened my notebook, quickly going over my notes, then recounted the events as they'd occurred.

"Ultimately, there was poor service throughout the evening," I informed him. "But, Mr. Whitman, a lot of that could've been forgiven if the wait staff hadn't been intentionally rude."

Elian listened then turned to our attorney. "I would like a moment to speak to my partner and attorney alone if you don't mind." Then he stood up and left the room, leaving the two other men with no choice but to follow.

Kristine and I sat silently for a moment, just absorbing what had happened, before Kristine finally whispered to our attorney, "What's this all about Chris?"

Chris just shrugged. "Not sure. It's not the older guy's M.O. Usually, they just demand the review be taken down and a public apology issued."

"Yeah, we already said we won't be doing that," Kristine cut in quickly.

"Of course, but we never got to that point. This could all just be a ploy. Stay vigilant," the attorney said as the door began to open.

Elian and their attorney came into the room – without Mr. Peady.

"I have a deal for you," Elian said, with a hint of a delicious Cuban accent flavoring his words. How had I not noticed that before? "I'll personally write a letter to you and your paper, apologizing for the bad service you received. You will publish my letter after you approve its contents, of course, along with another review of the restaurant for which I will not prepare my staff. My partner has just informed me he plans to sell out, so you should be able to get your review anonymously. I only request that you give me at least four weeks to make the necessary changes to the restaurant before you return."

Kristine looked at our attorney and when he nodded, she turned to Elian and accepted his offer.

As we rode back to the office, Kristine said, "You totally plan to go back before they expect you, right?"

"Of course," I nodded. "I also plan to find out what the guy's schedule is and show up when he isn't there."

"Good," Kristine replied. "It's probably best that I don't go with you this time since they'll coach the wait staff to be on the lookout for both you and I. Do you have a date you can take with you?"

"I can find one, I'm sure," I said, and we chuckled at our scheming.

"I'll tell you what, of all the things we do at the paper, this is the most entertaining," she confided, a grin still on her face.

"Speaking of entertaining," I replied, "did you catch the physique of that Cuban hunk?"

Kristine smirked at me. "I'm still breathing, aren't I? If he wasn't in the middle of a lawsuit against us, I'd have been laying on the flirtations heavily."

"I doubt it would've done you much good," I replied.

Kristine hit me on the arm. "I want you to know, I can woo a man as well as any other woman."

I laughed. "I don't doubt that for one minute, Kristine, but I seriously doubt you, or any woman for that matter, could woo that one. I'm almost sure he plays for my team."

Kristine stared at me for a moment. You could tell she was thinking about how the meeting had gone and the interactions with Elian. Then, she slapped her knee in frustration. "Damn, I think you're right. Damn, damn, damn. You'd think growing up in Miami, I'd have better gaydar." She sighed. "It sucks that the most beautiful men are gay. It just sucks, Martin."

"Ah, but do you have any idea how many gay men want to date a straight guy? It seems nobody is ever satisfied with what they've got." We both laughed and agreed that it was painfully true.

My friend Logan, who I'd met at a newspaper function, agreed to be my pretend date. He and I went to the restaurant and brewery just three weeks after the lawsuit meeting.

Logan and I had been on a couple of dates but soon figured out we were not compatible, so we'd decided to be friends instead. What Logan did like about me, though, was going on dates to restaurants around the city and sampling the food and giving his opinions about it.

I had done my own investigative work on Elian to see when he usually left work. There was no set schedule, and the man seemed to work long hours because he was almost always at the restaurant during lunch and dinner times.

On the few days I'd watched him, Elian never left before seven and often not until closing. During those nights of surveillance, I felt maybe he took his job a bit too seriously. I also thought more than once I was becoming a bit of a stalker and I was hardly paparazzi material.

Oh well, I excused my behavior as this was personal since his partner had pulled me into a lawsuit instead of dealing with his staff. I'd warned Logan that we'd have to meet early and wait for the big man to leave.

At seven, we were still sitting in my car, parked in a strategic place I'd found across the street. It allowed me the perfect view without being noticed. Luckily, my buddy was a gamer and didn't seem to notice we were sitting for so long in the car as he played with his phone. Fortunately, Elian left a little after seven.

As we walked in, I noticed some changes to the front of the restaurant. For one, the host's station now sat to the side, leaving a clear view of the brewery's huge machinery. While I'd had no beef with the décor, that change and some other subtle updates helped lighten the atmosphere. These changes certainly helped but mostly, I was here to evaluate the staff, the food, and the overall experience.

The restaurant was bustling, and one of three hostesses greeted us with a welcoming smile and chipper personality as we walked in the door. She efficiently informed us of a short wait for a table, and we were escorted to a spotless booth five minutes later. I smiled, and in my head, I logged the second point in their favor.

Within seconds, a server arrived at our table, smiled, and introduced himself before taking our drink orders. He returned just a moment later with them. So far, I was impressed. Even when I told him we'd changed our minds and both wanted a different drink, he wasn't frustrated by it. Again, he returned promptly with fresh drinks and also removed the half-empty beverages we'd been drinking without complaint while confirming they wouldn't be on the bill.

I'd been online, picking out what I wanted us both to order, and had prepped Logan, asking him to be picky but realistic.

Despite the fact that he asked for several changes to the meal he ordered, the server didn't miss a beat and never stopped smiling. He even suggested a better accompaniment to our dishes. Another point in their favor, I noted in my head.

The food arrived exactly as we'd ordered it, all well-cooked and still hot. After we started eating, I called the server back and asked about an appetizer we hadn't ordered that I claimed still hadn't arrived because I wanted to see how the server managed a customer who was lying. I found myself genuinely impressed. "I'm so sorry. I will have the kitchen put a rush on that," the server said, and quickly placed the new order with the kitchen. Either I wasn't as inconspicuous as I thought, or they had implemented some significant improvements.

I watched the customers and compared the service they were receiving to ours. As luck would have it, a couple seated just a few tables away changed their order three times, but the female server was exceedingly accommodating and even got the customer to laugh as she waited patiently for the order to be completed. When the couple's meals arrived, the young woman found a fault with something. Without complaint, the server whisked it back to the kitchen and five minutes later, the food came back cooked to the customer's satisfaction.

I smiled at Logan. "It's clearly not just us. They seem to have really turned things around."

Unfortunately, Logan had lost interest and was searching the dining room for what I assumed was pretty men. His conversation had changed from food to a critique of the different dating potentials. I laughed and told him how thankful I was that he'd helped me out tonight.

"Can I see your manager?" I asked the server when he returned with the credit card receipt. For the first time this evening, frustration crossed the server's face before he could conceal it.

"Yes, of course," he said and walked briskly toward the front of the restaurant.

Within seconds, the manager arrived at the table. "May I help you, sir?" he asked.

"Yes," I replied. "I was here a few weeks ago, and the service was awful. I swore I wouldn't return, but I decided to give you another chance, and I'm glad I did. Not only was my service impeccable, but I noticed the service to other customers was as well."

The manager, clearly surprised to have a positive review, went from shock to pride. "Thank you, sir. The owner recently made a lot of changes. It's rather encouraging to hear they have made enough of a difference that you would notice."

"Noticed, I have." I pulled my business card out of my shirt pocket and handed it to the manager. "You can tell Elian Whitman that he will receive a glowing review this time." I smiled as the manager's face turned pale.

"Thank you, um... sir," he squeaked out.

Logan laughed all the way home about the manager's nervous but proud expression.

I smiled over at him. "I imagine Whitman has put the fear of God into everyone that worked there, and as I wasn't supposed to show up until next week, they probably thought they were in the clear."

The next morning, I received an email from Elian. He explained that the restaurant had undergone a management change since the last review and that they were committed to providing the best service in the entertainment district. I was surprised he didn't mention the fact that my visit was a week early. I supposed that since I'd told the manager it was going to be a good review, he decided to let the slight go without comment. As promised, I wrote my second review. I included a description of the events that had led to another review this quickly after the first and submitted it, along with Elian's letter.

For the first time since arriving in Fort Lauderdale, my review went viral. We had hundreds of comments on the site. Almost everyone who wrote in confirmed the changes and gave the place five stars. The overall review had improved the restaurant's rating by a full point, moving it from three to four stars, which is a huge accomplishment for any restaurant.

I searched Google and TripAdvisor, and those reviews had improved as well. More than one person had mentioned the paper or Elian's letter. For a moment, I was the star of the *Fort Lauderdale Press*... well, at least until next week's edition.

A week after the review, another email arrived in my inbox from Elian. "I would like to meet you for coffee one morning, if you're available."

At first, I considered ignoring the email, but I thought this could be a good time to go over the changes and offer some beneficial feedback to the restaurant owner. I ran the idea by Kristine, and she agreed it would be fine. So, I wrote Elian back with my availability, along with a couple of my favorite coffee shops in the entertainment district.

Elian

Things were quite emotionally hot after the mediation. My co-owner, who owned significantly less than me, had threatened to sue me six ways to Sunday. But he was an ass, and he seemed to think suing was the solution to everything. I basically told him to do what he needed to do, but neither my family nor I would ever work with him again if he did.

We weren't what you'd call big money, but we were a name in the restaurant business. It must've been enough because the guy agreed to let me to buy him out.

I hated to tell him, but my family would never work with him again anyway. He was a loose cannon, and we'd learned long ago when those go off, it's best not to be holding any of the ammunition.

Now I needed to deal with that hunk who'd taken us to task over the lousy service. I've always liked a strong-willed man. And this guy didn't give an inch, and damn, if that wasn't hot as hell.

I wasn't that shocked that he'd shown up a week early, and to be honest, I sort of expected him to. He wasn't going to give us much leverage regarding his reviews. It appeared that when this guy put his name on something, it was with integrity. And dammit, if that wasn't another major turn-on for me.

After the glowing review, I wanted to celebrate and damned if I didn't want to celebrate with him. Sure, it's possible he was straight, but if the way he looked at me was any indication, he was bi at the very least. It couldn't hurt to test the boundaries with him. Besides, it would be fun to muss that perfect facade up a bit.

I sent him an email and did a little happy dance in my chair when I saw his response was yes.

The meeting happened late morning at a little coffee shop five blocks away from his restaurant. I intentionally dressed in jeans and a tight-fitting t-shirt. There was no need to come off as a total jerk, even though I must have seemed like that during our first meeting.

Martin met me with a smile, and before he sat down, asked, "You aren't here to kill me, are you?"

"No, that was last week when I learned you showed up a week early to review us."

Martin laughed out loud, transforming his serious face into a much younger version of himself. "Surely, you had to suspect I wouldn't just show up when you were prepared for me."

"No." I shook my head. "I assumed you'd be early, but I was hoping you wouldn't be."

"You have nothing to worry about. Your team did a fantastic job. I was genuinely impressed. Is that why you wanted to meet?"

I stared at him for a moment, trying to decide if I should be honest or not. If I chose not to be, though, I'd probably lose any hope of going out with the guy. "No, if I'm going to be honest, even under the circumstances of how we met, I wanted to ask you out."

I must have surprised him because he stared at me for several seconds too long.

"I'm sorry if you're straight, or if this is inappropriate. But, if you're interested, maybe now that the review is over, it wouldn't be inappropriate or awkward."

I knew I was babbling, but I didn't seem to be able to stop.

Martin continued to look at me, dumbfounded, until the barista called his name. He smiled at me and said, "Hold that thought." Then, he got up and walked over to the counter to pick up his latte.

By the time he returned, I'd gotten myself under control and was ready for his rejection, although what he said gave me hope.

He sat across from me, holding his latte. "I kinda think it is against the rules to date restaurant owners."

Noticing how he hadn't refused but rather stated it was against some rule, I nodded and smiled. "Well," I said, realizing my accent had become more pronounced, "I wouldn't want you to break the rules. Do you plan to review my restaurant again?"

"Not in the foreseeable future," he admitted.

"Do you plan to review anyone else in the brewery or any other business that could be in competition with mine?"

He thought for a few moments. "Yes, although I'm not sure which ones off the top of my head."

"Then," I replied, feeling a little smug, "since you're not reviewing me, unless you were to tell me when you were reviewing a competitor, I'm unsure where the conflict is." Thinking quickly, I also added, "And one more question, if I didn't own the brewery and were just asking you out on a date, would you say yes?" I felt like a teenage boy asking someone to the prom.

Martin thought for a moment. "I'd probably have said yes, if you weren't an owner in the area where I'm in charge of reviewing restaurants. However, unless you plan to sell up, I'm sorry but I'll have to say no."

I sat dumbfounded for a minute. I was trying to figure out how much I wanted to say. My attorneys would probably scalp me if they knew I was about to admit this. I took another look at the handsome man and decided to throw caution to the wind. "I will tell you something, but you'll have to write on that napkin next to you that you will not tell anyone what I'm going to say. God help me, you have to *swear* you will not write about this in your paper!"

"Agreed," he said. He reached into his briefcase, pulled out a notepad and pen, and ignoring the proposed napkin wrote, *For the next sixty days, I promise not to repeat anything told to me at this table without Elian's permission.*

"Will this work?" he asked, handing it to me.

I read over the note and smiled. "You don't miss a beat, do you?"

Martin smiled back. "I may be a food critic, but I'm also a reporter. I know how to protect a source, and I also know you need to ensure there are timelines. So, if that works, let's hear the news."

I scratched out the timeline he'd written and wrote over it *one-hundred and twenty days* and passed it back for him to sign. When he signed it along with the day's date, I began.

"I'm going to sell the brewery," I said after I folded his promissory note and placed it in my pocket. "In fact, the sale was just about to go through when your review came out. That's what made my partner so crazy. He was hoping to get you to retract your review with the threat of suing the paper. During the meeting, I saw you and your editor exchange looks, and I immediately realized two things. One, you weren't going to back down. And two, you were telling the truth. A prolonged legal battle would have ended the sale for good, so that's why I agreed to have you reassess and to write an apology letter myself.

"I was in Dallas when your review came out, closing a deal on a new restaurant there. It took another week for me to complete the purchase, and then I had to ensure my new staff were willing and able to survive without me. When I knew they were, I headed back to Fort Lauderdale to help Peady clear up the mess created by your painful, yet justified and honest review. That's why I wasn't at the initial meetings. Had I been, I'm sure I would have been able to resolve the issue before you had to come to a mediation with us."

Martin leaned forward showing he might be intrigued by my story. "So, you took the management over from Mr. Peady and instituted the improvements I saw?"

"Yes." I smiled. "Peady had some financial issues that needed to be resolved quickly. When we left the meeting, I agreed to buy him out, and after some interesting negotiations, the restaurant was all mine, so I stayed to fix it. Luckily, our attorney was present when Peady was throwing his fit outside the room. He was immediately able to put a contract together with the amount of money Peady wanted for the sale."

"Why is that lucky?" Martin asked.

I grinned at his question, thinking about everything I did after Peady went loco. Then there was the final contract that completely took Peady out from any further control over the business.

"Because after you gave us the glowing review that moved us from three to four stars, I got another offer on the place. This offer was for around fifty percent more than the other buyer had offered." I paused, smiling from ear to ear. When he didn't comment, I continued. "Your review hit us like a ton of bricks. But because of it, and because of the changes we made, you actually upped my profits significantly, and I will be increasing my profit without a partner to share the proceeds with. You, sir, are my good luck charm."

Martin

I was amazed by the conversation. I couldn't have cared less whether my review benefited Elian financially or not, but I was intrigued by the revelation, nonetheless. Finally, after mulling it over in my mind, I responded. "Elian, I'm very pleased things worked out for you, but until you sell the business, I'm afraid it's still a no on that date."

Elian appeared crestfallen. "I was sure the story would woo and convince you to go out with me." He recomposed himself quickly and continued. "My papa always said that the best things in life require the most effort. When things come to you with no effort, they tend to go as quickly as they came. So, I accept this challenge."

He picked up my hand and kissed it like you see men do in the old romance movies from the nineteen fifties and sixties and then grinned at me, and I swear I swooned just a bit at his beautiful expression. "Until the restaurant is sold, I will let you be, but as soon as it is, I'll be knocking on your door again." With that, he rose and left the little coffee shop.

I remained sitting, allowing myself time to finish my latte and pondering the man that had just left. I already knew I was attracted to Latin men. That was just how I was. Elian was not only beautifully put together, but the man had charm, charisma, and clearly a very well-tuned business savvy. *It might be fun to date him.*

I finished my latte, tossed the cup, and walked out to my car. I called Kristine on my way back to the office, wanting to catch her before she left for an assignment she'd warned me about. When she answered, I told her how Elian had asked me out, and she screamed into the phone.

"Oh, Martin, he is delicious," she said.

"Yes, he is, but Kristine, it would *not* look good for me to go out with a man I just gave a glowing follow-up review to."

"I agree, I agree," Kristine said. "And you have my most sincere admiration for your willpower. In fact, I'm glad you have that willpower, so I don't have to chastise you for doing something I would've said yes to the second he asked me out!"

I laughed at her honesty and secretly wished I'd thrown ethics to the wind and kissed the gorgeous man right where he sat. "Oh well," I said, concluding the conversation. "At least I have someone to fantasize about for a few months."

Elian

I was really attracted to the young food critic, but if he'd just said yes to my invite, I'd probably have had my way with him and lost interest. The fact that he was making me work for it piqued my curiosity.

Did that make me a cliché? Truth be told, I didn't really care if it did, I was a man who loved men. Being a restauranteur, I had plenty of gay men at my disposal, and I tended to go through them fairly quickly.

There'd been a few invitations since I'd met with the handsome Mr. Williams. I considered going out with them just to relieve the pressure, but for some reason, I couldn't get that man's face out of my head.

Instead of chasing the proverbial tail, I decided to put my nose to the grindstone and get the deal on the restaurant done. Besides, thanks to my former partner's screwups, the whole sale thing was weeks behind, and I still had the Dallas restaurant to get back to. I needed to get my act together, whether Martin was in the picture or not.

As fate would have it, the buyer was anxious to get his hands on the restaurant. So, when the title company and attorneys both said they were done early, I jumped at the chance to get the deal. We both came in and signed our paperwork, completing the sale two full months earlier than we'd planned.

I sent a large flower arrangement to Martin with a note that read, *The deal is done. The ink is drying, so I hope to get that date we talked about.*

Martin

Although there was no signature, I knew exactly who the flowers were from. Shortly after they arrived, Kristine showed up at my office door. "Are they from him?"

"They are, and I'll give you a scoop. I told him he couldn't ask me out again until he didn't own the restaurant."

Kristine's eyes grew huge. "Did he sell the restaurant?"

"I'm not at liberty to answer that," I replied. "But you owe me big-time, Kristine, if the sale turns into a big story!"

"Yes, I do," she replied as she turned back toward her office, eager to put someone on the story. She stopped just as she got to the door and turned back around. "So, did he ask?"

"Not yet," I said as I pointed toward the huge flower arrangement. "I don't think that came with a question, but I have no doubt it's coming."

"Oh, I love a love story," she said. Then, she stopped, and with a serious face, added, "But you know, I'm always going to be jealous you got that hunk of a man. Always, Martin... always!"

I laughed as she disappeared down the walkway toward her office.

It was the next day that I got a call from Elian. He asked if I'd meet him at a little community bar on Las Olas Beach. Elian must have figured out it wasn't part of the area I did reviews in. This time, I didn't hesitate in telling him I'd love to.

Elian informed me he had to go back to Dallas for a week but that he'd like to meet me before he left, and we agreed on a time. Then, when the call ended, I rushed down to Kristine's office.

Her door was closed, but through her door's window, I could see she was chatting with one of her reporters. She glanced up, and when I winked at her, she grinned and waved back.

When her meeting was over, she knocked on my door and came straight in. "So, did he call?"

"Yep," I replied.

"And you said yes?" she asked.

"Yep," I replied again.

"Damn you," she said, then hugged me. "I don't know if I'm more happy or jealous. Either way, I want all the details after I'm done with this next meeting. We are going out to lunch... you're buying."

It was difficult to tell who was more excited about the upcoming date, me or Kristine.

I accused her of living vicariously through me, and she hit me on the arm. "Yeah, when you're a workaholic, overachiever who works twenty-four hours a day, seven days a week, you have to get your thrills through other people's lives. Why do you think I became a reporter?"

"We're going to have to start fixing you up with hot men, boss," I replied. I only used the term *boss* when I was being belligerent, or about to do something she wouldn't approve of.

"Oh no! I need to date as much as I need to be hit by a bus."

I rolled my eyes in response, dropping the subject, but both of us knew I hadn't dropped it permanently. Kristine tried to argue the point further, but I just smiled and enjoyed watching how much that wound her up. Finally giving up, she changed the subject to work, clearly hoping to dissuade me from thinking along those lines any longer.

I drove down to Las Olas Beach, to the destination chosen by Elian. As I drove, I was reminded how little I actually went to the beach. When I first got the job, I thought I'd live at the beach, but instead, I depressingly spent most of my time at the paper, and perusing restaurants or nightlife in the entertainment district.

When I arrived at the parking spot Elian texted me was open, I had to give credit to a guy who thought about the little things like setting up a parking spot for his date. Just as I did with the restaurants I was reviewing, I began to mentally calculate points for our time together.

I walked across the road to the restaurant where Elian had asked me to meet him. I found him exactly where he said he'd be, sipping what appeared to be a martini, and after greeting me warmly, asked what I was drinking.

I'd nervously searched for what drinks to order on a first date as I prepared for the night.

"Gin and tonic," I replied, although I seriously hated gin and tonic!

Elian

Martin was dressed in jeans that accented his slim, muscular legs and a nice button-down that showed off his slight upper body. The contrast was maybe a bit odd but very sexy.

He asked me how my Dallas project was progressing, and I shook my head, exasperated. "It's going to be fine as a business, but I'm afraid in regard to my aspirations, it's another dead end."

Martin smiled as the server dropped off the gin and tonic.

"I'm looking for a diamond in the rough," I told him.

"What do you mean?" Martin asked.

"You know there are hundreds of budding restaurants all across the country, but only one in a million has a strong enough business model to become a successful national franchise. That is what I want... that something special."

Martin shook his head. "I guess I don't know much about the business side of restaurants. I just know the food and service side. So, what makes a restaurant a potential for franchise?" Martin asked.

I shook my head. "It isn't what makes them able to be a franchise. Any business can technically do that. It's what makes a business *successful* as a franchise."

Martin shrugged. "Business was never my forte. In college, I was required to take a business class along with my journalism degree because, as my advisor informed me, if I was going to be a journalist, I had to understand the background of a business. Unfortunately for me, the business class was the one C grade I got, bringing an otherwise stellar GPA down a notch." Martin laughed at the memory. "My ridiculous advisor even recommended I retake the class, but I told him I'd rather take the C than go through that torture again."

I smiled, taking this revelation as my cue to change the subject. But before I could, Martin asked me, "So, you're buying restaurants, trying to find one you can franchise?" Then, he shuddered as he asked, "Like McDonald's?"

I chuckled. "No, not exactly. I buy restaurants that have potential. I improve them, but if they don't pan out as having long-term potential for expansion, I sell them. That is how I came to be sitting across from you. The restaurant with the attached brewery seemed to have potential, but the structure was lacking the luster I thought it might have."

"So," Martin stated unenthusiastically, "you sold it and made a profit."

I turned to him curiously. "Do you not approve then?"

Martin shook his head. "It isn't that I approve or disapprove, but a restaurant that can pump out the same old same old, day in and day out is boring and, to use your own terms, lacks any luster a diamond may have. If you're asking me if I approve of franchises, the answer is it isn't something I care for. Still, if you're asking if I approve of taking a quality restaurant and turning it into something fantastic that you can then sell like you did the brewery, I can't really begrudge you that."

I took a drink and leaned back, before turning to Martin again, this time in an inquisitive way that seemed to make him uncomfortable.

"You really do care about the industry, don't you?" I asked, feeling surprised by my revelation.

"Yes, why would I be in this job if I didn't? Good quality food with exceptional service can be the backdrop of family memories. Relationships can start, become stronger, and even end based on how well a restaurant functioned. It isn't really a business to me as much as it is a lifestyle," Martin explained.

"Everything you say is true, but more restaurants go under than any other business venture started in America. Without a strong business plan, a restaurant can't survive."

Just as I made my last statement, I could see the shutters coming down over Martin's eyes. If I didn't change tactics fast, I was going to lose my chances with this guy, and I'd already worked harder to talk him into this date than I had anyone, well, ever!

"Okay," I said with as much gusto as I could muster. "Enough business talk, let's go see the sights.

I have some things planned that I think, well, I *hope*, that you'll like."

Martin smiled broadly, clearly relieved the business talk had ended.

Martin

Elian paid for both drinks, took my hand, and led me out the door. I admit, I thought this was very odd. I was from Texas, and even though my ex had been affectionate, holding a man's hand in public wasn't something I did without thinking about it first, but apparently, this wasn't the case for Elian. Considering we were on Las Olas Beach in Fort Lauderdale, I couldn't think of a reason to pull my hand back, so I decided to just let it rest in Elian's.

He led me down to the beach, walking along the surf, allowing the water to lap up onto his sandals.

I'd worn shoes, so I didn't really want to walk in the waves, but Elian seemed to know where the surf was going to land and managed to keep me dry, at least for the most part.

After walking quietly for several minutes, we came to a set of little shacks that backed up to some of Fort Lauderdale's older condos off the beach.

I looked up at them and said aloud, "It is a miracle these haven't been bought and torn down and replaced with the larger, bigger varieties."

"Not much chance of that, at least not anytime soon," Elian replied. "These belong to Raul Alverez, who built them himself in the early nineteen nineties. He considers them his masterpieces and treasures them like they are his children. He'll have to be dead and in his grave before they get sold to a developer who'd tear them down."

"Do you know this Alverez?" I asked.

Elian's face lit up, "He's my uncle. Now, come with me, I have a treat for you."

I was momentarily surprised by the revelation and returned my vision back to the three condominiums lining the exclusive area of the beach. They were a reinterpretation of the Art Deco period.

I guessed there were ten to twelve floors, which in the early ninties would've been really tall for the area. Since then, lumbering giants had replaced all but these three buildings.

Part of me immediately liked that this Alverez had held out. The architecture was significantly more pleasing than what I saw on either side of them.

"What made your uncle choose this design?" I asked.

"Ah, good question," Elian replied. "My family moved here from Key West. They lived down there during the time of Ernest Hemingway. They owned several businesses up until the end of the nineteen eighties. My uncle went to the university to study architecture, but just before he finished, my grandfather passed away. Mi abuela, my grandma," he quickly interpreted, "couldn't handle the businesses by herself, and my mother was already married to my father and had moved to Seattle with him. My uncle was faced with the difficult decision between returning to Key West to help mi abuela or finishing school. Being raised to take care of family first, he decided to go home, but when he arrived, she'd already sold the businesses and the buildings. She told him she wanted him to have his dream, not his papa's dream, and selling the business allowed him to finish school without feeling like he was letting her down."

"Wow, that's pretty selfless of her," I replied, genuinely impressed with his grandmother.

Elian sighed, "Yeah, but she loved Key West. When I was little, she'd tell the story of Hemingway stopping by the bakery where her mama worked. While he ate a pastelito de guayaba and sipped on a caffe misto, she would sit across from him, asking hundreds of kid questions, which she said he would answer as if they were important questions asked by one of the magazines that reported about him. Her mother would eventually see her sitting with Mr. Hemingway and come to shoo her away, but he would always wink at her when her mama turned her back.

"She married my grandfather, mi abuelo, when she was seventeen. They had gone to school together, but he was a couple of years older than her. Abuela was poor, and he was wealthy, but that didn't stop them. With her help, they turned their corner store into a business anyone would be proud of. So, when Abuelo died, she made a good amount of money on the sale."

Elian stared wistfully out toward the sea. Even though I'd just met him, I could tell how much he'd loved his grandmother.

After a moment he continued speaking. "My uncle finished school and married my aunt who was from here. She convinced him to move his mother to Fort Lauderdale and build his buildings on land she had inherited from her family." As he explained, he pointed to the lots where the three buildings stood.

"Mi abuela wasn't very keen on leaving Key West. She was getting older and didn't want to leave her friends and family, so to convince her, tío–sorry, that means my uncle–drew up designs that mimicked old Key West. Abuela, of course, loved the drawings and told him, if he built these, she would move to Fort Lauderdale to live.

"The nineteen nineties were bustling times for Fort Lauderdale. Buildings were popping up around his property, so when he went to the bank with his drawings and plans, they didn't even blink an eye. He got the money, hired his brother-in-law, who was a well-respected contractor in the area, and built the buildings in record time."

I continued to stare at the buildings, more intrigued by them now than I'd been before. "I admit, I'm a sucker for these kinds of stories. Did your grandmother move here as she promised?" I asked.

"Sí, she did, and loved being here. Before long, my mama and papa returned to Fort Lauderdale too and bought one of my uncle's condos. In fact, when I'm in town this is where I stay."

"Nice," I said, more to myself than him.

"Here is the best part," Elian said, pointing to the cluster of buildings at the base of the condos I'd noticed when we first walked up. "These were my father's idea. Before there were food trucks, my father liked and promoted the idea of tiny restaurants that could shift with the interest of the public.

"He convinced my uncle and aunt to allow him to build the buildings that you see, and then marketed them to various restaurants in the area to sell food to the beachgoers. As with anything, there was resistance to the newness of the idea. Even though he ended up not renting them out, he opened his own restaurants here. He had a pizza parlor here." Elian pointed to the red and white building to his left. "This was my restaurant because, as a teenage boy, I was obsessed with pizza.

"The little white building was a burger place, which did well enough that my papa opened several around town. Have you heard of Whitman Burgers?"

"Wow, really?" I exclaimed. I had eaten there a few times because sometimes you just want a greasy burger.

Elian smiled and pointed toward another building. "The little green building, as you can see, is an ice cream shop, and my mama still runs this herself, but of course, with a lot of outside help.

"Now, this black and grey building just over to the end of the property, that is something special. This is the place I have brought you to eat, and I am excited to get your opinion."

We could hear the laughter before we walked inside the small building, which was standing room only. The smell that hit me immediately caused my mouth to water. I recognized the traditional Cuban smells, and since Cuban has some one of my favorite dishes, I was excited to try.

When Elian came in behind me, the lady at the front gave him a nasty look. "You should be helping your sister, not running around town like a tomcat." When she noticed me standing next to him, she blushed.

"Do not mind me," she yelled my way. "I'm just angry because my brother is supposed to be half owner, which he thinks means he only has to do half the work."

"And this is my sister, Lucia. Lucia, stop grumbling for half a second, and come meet Martin. He is a food critic."

Lucia stopped short, turned her full attention on her brother, then to me. "I hope you didn't bring him here to get special attention," she said. By then, most of the people in the restaurant had turned to look at us.

I turned to Elian as well, waiting for him to explain why he had brought me to this place where the food smelled like heaven, then set me up to either be treated with hostility or more likely driven out of the place entirely.

Elian grinned naughtily and whispered, "Trust me, this will be fun. Lucia, this poor man has been eating food at the restaurants in the entertainment district. He has never eaten real Cuban, only the food they try to pass as Cuban down there. Can't you be a dear and show him what real food tastes like?"

Both Lucia and I glowered at Elian. She quickly glanced at a man who was serving a couple at the end of a long bar and said, "Mi corazón, please find a seat outside for mi hermano y el critico."

The man turned toward Elian and shook his head before saying, "Right away, mi amor."

He quickly finished with his customers, then dragged Elian and me outside onto a paved patio. "Why do you have to come in and antagonize your sister like that?" he asked.

"Because she is too full of herself, Manuel, and it is my brotherly duty to keep her down to earth."

"If you keep antagonizing her, especially when she is four months pregnant, you may find yourself under the earth. Be warned, cuñado."

Elian laughed heartily. "Por favor, cuñado, I want you to bring my guest the number fourteen, and me the number twelve. Martin, what would you like to drink?" he asked.

"I have no idea what you just ordered for me, so I don't know. You can order that as well."

Elian thought for a moment while Manuel went back inside to tell his wife our orders. "Do you prefer wine or beer?" he asked.

"Depends on the menu. If I'm eating at an upscale restaurant where the food is delicate and light, I tend to go with a glass of white wine, but when I'm eating more hearty foods, such as dishes with beef, I tend to prefer a red. When I'm eating more down-home, I usually go for a beer, but the flavor also depends on what is being served."

"What do you usually drink when you are eating Cuban?" he asked.

"Chicken or beef?" I returned.

"Chicken *and* beef," he replied.

I thought for a moment. "Do you have Cristal?" I asked.

Elian turned toward me with a shocked expression. "Sí, but most Americans don't usually know what that is. How do you know Cristal?"

I was pleased to have shocked my arrogant date and responded, "My mother and I took a vacation to Havana with the first tour group that went. Cristal was what they served at every restaurant we went to. I later learned it was because it was the most expensive beer they sell, and they could get us unwary tourists to buy it."

Elian laughed, "I think a Cristal will pair well with what I ordered you. Now, forgive me a moment, but I'm going to go get your beer and let Manuel wait on paying customers."

When he returned, he had a white wine in one hand and my beer in the other. "My sister will literally yell at me when our food is done. I told Manuel he didn't need to babysit us, so if you need something, just let me know."

As promised, Lucia yelled out the door that Elian needed to come get his order before she threw it at him. I could hear several people laugh at her threat. From what I could tell, the angry sprite would likely make good on her threat if he pushed her too far. Elian smiled at me and dashed in to get our food.

When he returned, Manuel walked out the door behind Elian, and both had their hands full of food. "What on earth did you order?" I asked.

"Pretty much everything on the menu," Elian replied. "I hope you're hungry."

I was hungry, but I doubted I'd ever been *this* hungry. There was enough food here to feel the entire city. When Elian settled, he placed an empty plate in front of me and another in front of himself.

"This is family-style. Just promise me you will try each item, and give me your honest opinion."

I was beginning to have second thoughts about this. I was never one to mix business and pleasure, and I didn't want to critique a meal that had been cooked by my date's sister, especially on a first date.

I was preparing my escape when Elian said, "You can be brutally honest. I promise not to get angry with you. Your honest opinion is all I'm asking."

I began to wonder if this was to promote his sister's business. *Damn,* I thought, *well, better to make the best of it and get done as soon as possible.*

I cut a piece of chicken from the plate directly in front of me, and when I put it in my mouth, my eyes literally watered from the beautifully seasoned meat. Before I could help myself, I moaned with pleasure.

Elian watched me, clearly enjoying my response. Without speaking, he dipped a fork into the black beans to my right and dapped a helping onto my plate.

When I scooped some into my mouth, the same sensation of perfectly seasoned flavor exploded on my tongue.

I loved black beans and ate them often, but these were different. The herbs she'd used perfectly complemented the earthy flavor of the beans. I mostly ignored Elian through the meal, tasting each dish and moaning with pleasure as I sampled them. The food was certainly the best Cuban food I'd had in Fort Lauderdale, and likely, the best ever.

When I'd eaten all I could handle, I leaned back, took a draw of my Cristal beer, then smiled at my date.

"So?" Elian asked. "What were your thoughts?"

"I think we both know I enjoyed it," I responded.

Elian grinned. "You are a food critic, surely you can come up with more descriptive language than that."

I gave Elian a nasty look, then said, "The chicken was moist, perfectly charred, and the seasoning on it, and every other dish, was beautifully done. In some way—I'm not exactly sure how—the beef in the ropa vieja melted in your mouth, and the pastelitos de carne were perfect. I usually avoid those because they tend not to have enough flavor for me or they are over-seasoned, but your sister's was spot-on—a perfect mix of the seasoned meat and flaky crust. What I'm most impressed with is consistency. You basically ordered twenty-five dishes here, and everything was equally delicious. I could eat at any of the star-rated restaurants in Fort Lauderdale, and I doubt they'd provide the same level of consistency across the entire menu or provide speedy service at the same time. If you brought me here to get a good review, although I think it is bad form to pretend like you wanted a date, I will gladly write up my review and pass it to my colleague that covers this part of town."

I hadn't noticed that Lucia had come out of the restaurant to collect the dishes. "You will do no such thing. I can barely handle the foot traffic as it is, I will not have you writing any damned thing in the paper just to run me over with a whole crowd of new customers. Thank you for your compliments, but I am happy being the size that I am."

"Lucia," Elian chuckled, "he isn't here as a critic. He's here as my date. I just wanted him to see we aren't just about making money. We also love the food."

She put the plates she had just picked up back on the table, turned to me, and said, "I don't know what my brother has told you, but we are first and foremost a restaurant that serves high quality food and service. I run my business as I see fit and do not let money rule us. This is why my brother will never take this place and turn it into one of his fancy business schemes, and if you are here to promote that, you and I will have problems." She picked up the plates again and headed into the kitchen with her head held high.

Elian roared with laughter as soon as the door closed behind his sister. "I have been trying to convince Lucia to allow me to turn this concept into a franchise since we were teenagers. She will have nothing to do with it and told me if I force the issue, she will quit and take all her recipes with her. I know the two women who work with her are fiercely loyal, so without Lucia, there is no Lucia's.

"So why did you bring me here?" I asked, perplexed.

"Because you think I am only about business and money. You needed to see that I am also about family and that my family values the same things you said you do. I may be a businessman, but family comes first."

I couldn't help but stare at my date. The man had shocked me first with exquisite food, then with a full contradiction of who I thought he was. "So, if your sister relented and said she would work with you, would you exploit her?"

"First, let's be clear that Lucia will go to her grave before she would be willing to relent to anything I want her to do. Second, even *if* she would consider my offer, I wouldn't, no. I know without a shadow of a doubt, Lucia does this because she loves it. It feeds her soul, and she expresses her love in this way. I would never take that love away from her, nor would I eliminate the very best place to eat Cuban food outside of Cuba."

"Okay you win," I said, shaking my head. "I did think you were a self-absorbed businessman who could only think about the bottom line. Our conversation earlier when we met made me think you were looking for the next business to exploit, but clearly, you are only a self-absorbed businessman who will exploit strangers."

Laughter erupted behind Elian as Lucia rounded the back of the building toward the little outdoor table. "Okay," she said, clearly having heard my comment to Elian, "I like this one, let me bring you some dulce de leche. Here I thought you were just one of his prudish business friends." She then disappeared back into the building before Elian caught his breath.

"Wait." I tried to stop her. I was so full I had no idea where more food would go.

"You won't win now. She likes you, so she will never rest until you are fat and plump. Besides, I never get to eat her dulce de leche. If you don't want it, I'll eat it."

Once again, I glowered at my date. I might have found a few redeeming qualities in the man, but he was insufferable, to say the least.

The dulce de leche was in a category of its own. Once again, I'd sampled many like this over the years, but if I had to critique this one, I would write that it was something special, something better, and shouldn't be classified in the same category as the others I'd eaten.

As promised, Elian ate most of the dulce, eating it quickly and not savoring it, which annoyed me. With that much delicate flavor, it should be savored.

After we finished, Elian took the remaining dishes into the kitchen, hugged his sister, and waved at Manuel. "Adiós, mi hermana. It was as good as usual," he said as we left.

I thought I saw Lucia flip Elian off as he walked out the door, but the door frame was in the way, and I couldn't be sure. Dispite the fact he embodied the word insufferable, I couldn't resist the idea of getting to know him more. Unlike with Peter, my ex whose mom hated me on sight, Lucia seemed to like me more than she did her brother. *That could be a refreshing change,* I thought.

I hesitated after I walked out of the restaurant, and Elian immediately pulled my arm into his as we began walking back down the beach toward my car.

"Were you planning to bring me to your sister's tonight?" I asked.

"No," Elian chuckled. "I usually avoid mixing my dates with my family as they can be a lot to deal with, but you were getting the wrong impression of me, and

I needed you to see there is more to my personality than business. It needs to be well-balanced to be right. Next time, I'll take you to my favorite hamburger stand on the other side of Las Olas."

I stopped and looked at him. "Your favorite isn't the one your family owns?"

"Oh, no, not even close. My cousin runs that, and he couldn't cook to save his life *or* someone else's."

I laughed for the first time that evening. "So, it isn't just family you are obligated to. You also appreciate good flavor."

"Absolutely," Elian agreed. "If my sister's food wasn't the flavor worthy of feeding the gods, I would love her but never eat there. As such, I love my cousin but avoid his cooking."

We walked companionably back to my parking spot, and when we got to my car, Elian reached around and opened it for me. I was going to get in my car and leave to avoid the man until I felt a little more settled about him. Before I could escape, though, Elian reached over and kissed me gently on the lips, then whispered in Spanish, "Hasta la próxima vez guapo," and then in

English, "Until next time, handsome." And he left me staring after him.

The next morning, as I walked through the cubicles toward my office, several snickers crept up as I walked by. When I finally arrived at my office, I stopped short at the sight of several helium-filled balloons so big they barely fit. On the other side of the balloons, I saw my editor, Kristine, sitting in my office chair, smiling like the Cheshire Cat. I sighed and walked in.

"Morning, Kristine."

"Morning, sunshine. So, it appears someone got lucky last night."

I replied in a monotone voice, "We didn't have sex, if that's what you are implying."

"Martin," Kristine replied, "a man does not send balloons the day after a date unless the sex was good."

"Unless he didn't get sex *yet*," I corrected.

"Oh, even better," she said, getting up from my chair. "You are playing hard to get."

I sat in the vacated chair and rubbed my head.

"No, nothing like that. He didn't offer, and it would've been weird if he had. We went to his sister's restaurant down on Las Olas Beach, and afterward, he walked me back to my car, gave me a PG–rated kiss, and sent me on my way."

"I'm confused," Kristine joked. "Aren't gay men supposed to have sex first, then romance later?"

"Nice stereotyping," I said dryly. "I guess this man is a little different, or he isn't really attracted and just wants me for my ratings."

Kristine choked a bit from that comment. "Doubtful," she added, "considering I followed up on that lead, and he has indeed sold the restaurant."

"Don't be so sure," I said. "This guy is a businessman through and through. We don't know what his motives are yet. He sold that business, but it is more likely than not he has his eye on another in the area. It would be in his best interest to have a food critic in his back pocket."

Kristine scrunched up her face and said, "You are jaded, Martin Williams. What happened to you to cause someone your age to be so jaded?"

I glanced up at her and responded, "You know very well why I'm jaded about men. Besides, I learned long ago that not all men are what they appear to be on the surface."

Kristine studied me for a moment. "From your editor's perspective, I'm very happy you are watching your back and avoiding a scandal with someone who may be manipulating you for a good review. From a friend's perspective, I hate to see you pass up an opportunity to have fantastic sex with a very hot man just because you were burned in the past."

I smiled weakly at my friend as she turned and left.

Since I'd driven away from Elian, I'd decided I would not go out with him again, even if he asked. There was too much in the way of our success. Not only was the man a serial restaurateur, but he very likely had a hidden agenda. I swore after Peter I'd be more vigilant when it came to men, and this one threw up every red flag.

Admittely, I liked the idea of his uncle who refused to sell the deco-inspired condos and his sister who ran the restaurant down on Las Olas for the sole reason of doing what she loved, but just because he had good family didn't mean he wasn't the *bad seed* of the bunch.

A week passed before I heard from Elian again. It was Friday evening, and I'd just gotten off work and was walking to my car when I saw him leaning against it, all smiles.

"You appear to have just eaten a canary. Why are you leaning on my car?" I asked, unable to hide my frustration with him showing up.

Elian's face dropped. "You really don't trust me, do you?"

As I stood in front of him, I decided to answer honestly. "I don't trust easily and it's very possible you have ulterior motives."

Elian smiled again. "But you must trust someone eventually, so it might as well be me. What are your plans tonight?" he asked.

"Work, TV, and bed—in that order," I replied.

"You live a wild and crazy life, Martin. Come with me. I just got back in town, and I'd like to have you join me down at the beach. Tonight is a special party. There will be lots of people there. Free booze and lots of dancing."

With his comment about dancing, Elian did a little move that demonstrated just how Caribbean he really was. The subtle movement struck me right in the groin area. I always did have a thing for Latin men, but throw just the slightest mix of Caribbean sex appeal into the mix, and I was toast.

I thought about the conversation with Kristine. I was jaded, and I knew that belonged to my ex's betrayal. It really wasn't fair to any man, be it Elian or a future date, to compare him to someone from my past.

I looked Elian in the eye for a moment, trying to see any signs of an ulterior motive before responding. Elian's smile never faded.

"Okay, maybe," I said, "but let's get this boundary firmly set. I will go with you tonight, and if I continue to like you, then I might go out with you again. But let's be very clear: if you ask me even one time to write a review for you or to help find someone who will give you a positive review on your restaurants, then I'm out. I'll disappear, and I will not respond to anything you write to me again. If you are buttering me up for business reasons, you should stop now and save us both a lot of trouble."

"La gusta a él!" Elian said and turned a circle with his hands in the air. I had had enough Spanish in high school and college to know he'd said something to the affect that I liked him.

"That is all you got from my lecture?" I asked with a chuckle.

Elian put his hands on my elbows and said, "You think I have ulterior motives, but I don't. I want to go out with you, and get to know you—maybe woo you a little—but I don't need or want you to make my business better. I can do that on my own."

Then Elian kissed me on the lips, lingering a little longer than he had the previous time. Still no tongue, but I couldn't deny there was plenty of passion there.

"So, you will go with me to the party?" he asked.

I sighed but smiled in spite of myself. "Sure, I'll go with you to the party."

Elian all but danced around me as we made plans to meet in one hour at my apartment.

I rushed home and changed into party attire—black shirt that tapered along my torso, accompanied by tight jeans that hugged my waist and legs. When Janice recently visited me, she called this my "push me down into the pillows and fuck me outfit." Since then, every time I put this outfit on, I'd giggle.

I was beginning to get excited about the party. It'd been too long since I let myself go out just for the sake of dancing and having fun. I had to admit, the talk with Elian had alleviated some of my concerns. I was beginning to like this guy, but I still didn't totally trust him, and I was nowhere ready to let my guard down.

Despite that, I convinced myself to just go have some fun. Free booze and a night of dancing seemed like just what I needed to unwind. Who knows? If the Cuban prince played his cards right, he might even get more than just a peck on the mouth. I might even French kiss him. "God forbid," I said aloud, giggling.

I laughed at the thought of being so restrained. This would be the first time I'd been on a second date with a guy and not have at least put my tongue down his throat. Janice would have told me this is some kind of sign.

Thinking of Janice, I texted her, "Going out with a gorgeous, sexy Cuban to a beach party. I'll send you a picture when he arrives to pick me up."

Janice texted back immediately with a picture of a hot redhead who appeared to be rather shocked and a bit disheveled in the picture. "This is my date—hunky man who I'm currently seducing. Let's talk tomorrow." Then, a few seconds later, she texted, "Tomorrow evening." I laughed out loud at the text. The poor guy had no idea what he was in for. Janice was nothing if not intense.

Elian arrived still dressed in the jeans and t-shirt he was in when we met in the parking lot. When he stepped out of the car, I glared at him suspiciously and said, "You don't appear to be dressed for a party."

He looked me up and down and whistled. "You, however, look like you're not planning to stay long at the party." When Elian's eyes met mine, his normal cool had been replaced with hunger and need. The intensity in his expression made me blush. "Should I go change?" I asked.

Elian responded immediately with "No... no, no, I want to watch you in that outfit all night. Then, I want to..." He stopped himself before he went on. "It is probably best that I not finish that statement. I will need to go by the apartment and change before we head to the party."

The raw sexuality that I'd seen in Elian's gaze had turned every warning signal on in my head, but it also sparked every sexual need in me. So, instead of responding in my usual smart-assed way, I simply replied, "Okay."

We got into Elian's little sports car and sped off toward Las Olas Beach. I was deposited in a small bar inside his uncle's first condo as Elian disappeared up the elevator. He returned before I had finished the gin and tonic he'd quickly ordered for me before disappearing, and was dressed to the nines. His sports coat was perfectly tailored to show off his muscular build, and like me, he wore jeans that accented *every* aspect of his body.

I smiled when he arrived and said, "That is a bit of a change." I stood up, and taking the initiative, laid a thick kiss on him—certainly not the pecks he'd given me. I wanted to be clear I had some initiative in me as well. Elian wasn't going to be the only one running this show.

The kiss was hotter than I'd anticipated, and when I finally pulled back, Elian's eyes were a mix of shock and lust. "Now," I replied, "I think I'm ready for this party."

A very attractive man who appeared to be in his sixties came over and said, "What kind of party are you throwing, Elian?" Elian turned to the man and stammered a bit before he said, "Tío, this is my date, Martin Williams. Martin, this is my uncle, Raul Alverez." Elian appeared to be both embarrassed and deeply affected by the kiss.

I knew it was naughty, but I was enjoying the smooth player's reaction more than I probably should've. It was the first time I'd seen the cool, unmovable demeanor of the Cuban prince disturbed.

I smiled at the gentleman and said, "Hello, señor Alverez. It is my pleasure to meet you. Your nephew has told me truly remarkable things about you."

The man seemed to also be enjoying his nephew's discomfort as well and grabbed my hand in a strong, competent handshake. "This is the first time our boy has brought us someone to meet. It seems you have made an impression on him."

Elian's look alternated between his uncle and me—clearly not sure how to respond—but when he regained his composure, he said, "I've been away for work, but I wanted to spend some more time with

Martin, so I thought I'd ask him to join me at Mama and Papa's anniversary party. I doubt they'll mind."

Anniversary party? I thought. *No one said anything about an anniversary party.* I pinned Elian with a confused, wary look, which Elian's uncle noticed. "I take it the young man didn't realize it was a family gathering you brought him to?"

I decided to respond before Elian. "He seemed to have left that part out, but I'm excited to spend the evening with your family. I already met your niece, Lucia, and we seem to have hit it off. I'm sure I'll enjoy meeting the rest of you." This made the older man smile.

The party was a blast. I'd been to family gatherings of my other friends from Cuba and knew they could be very large and expansive affairs. This one, however, appeared more like a multi-generational beach party.

Elian's mother radiated eligant beauty, making it obvious where Elian and Lucia got their looks. His father's handsome features complemented his wife's; they made a beautiful couple, and judging by the ever-expanding crowd, a beloved one as well.

When we arrived at the beach, the party had already begun. It seemed hundreds of people lined the beach. Lucia and Manuel were working the food line, and a young man who was a muscular version of Manuel was behind the bar. I assumed he had to be Manuel's brother, which Elian confirmed when he went over to get us both a drink from the bar.

Elian waited at least an hour after we arrived to introduce me to his parents. His mother smiled when she saw me and reached out a graceful hand. "It is unusual for our Elian to bring a date to meet his family. Maybe he thought you would be less intimidated by us in a crowd." She winked at her son, then laughed when he squirmed.

The sound of her laugh paralyzed me for a moment, taking me back to when my ex's hateful mother attacked me. The painful memory hit me full-on, and I was sure I paled in response.

Elian's father must've noticed and said, "We love teasing our son, young man. You are welcome here, and we are very happy Elian brought you to play with us on our happy occasion."

Elian's mother must have caught her husband's tone as she, too, turned to me and smiled a happy, genuine smile, saying, "Don't mind me, love, I've had way too many toasts, and it is so enjoyable to tease my Elian." She mussed her son's perfectly combed hair and grinned at him. "We are exceptionally pleased you are here." She leaned over and kissed me square on the lips.

Elian pulled me away and said, "My mama is sloshed. She will be mortified tomorrow when Papa tells her that she kissed you like that."

When it was clear everyone had eaten, Manuel and Lucia came out from behind the buffet line and began dancing with the crowd. I was hesitant to dance, not knowing Elian's family, but after Manuel's muscle-bound brother soaked me with several drinks he was taking to a table I was standing beside, I let my inhibition slip away. I ended up dancing with a number of people I'd never met before. My experience with men was that they came and went. I figured it was unlikely Elian would last long, so I thought I might as well enjoy the party and let my hair down for a moment.

At one point, Lucia came up behind me and slipped her arms around my waist from behind. "My mama and papa said they like you. That is a good sign, mi amigo," she said. "Mi hermano must really like you to bring you to meet us on such a special occasion. How do you feel about mi hermano?" We danced as she talked, and I—who was not good at keeping my opinion to myself even when sober—had been drinking since I arrived.

"He is dashingly handsome," I said. "Too handsome to trust this early in the relationship."

Lucia laughed so hard at that comment she almost fell to the ground. I turned around and reached over to steady her. "Tu puedes ser la pareja perfecta de mi hermano," she said, and then danced away from me.

Despite my pitiful understanding of Spanish, I understood what Lucia had said: "You are the perfect match for my brother."

I doubted that I was anyone's perfect match. That was another lesson I learned from my past relationship; you can't assume you are someone's match. They will always surprise you. The sour thoughts took root in my mind, and I quickly needed space to process them. I slipped away from the party and found a nice round post to sit on several yards down the beach and a good distance from the party.

I'd always enjoyed hearing the laughter and music of a party on the beach, but I also enjoyed being away from it as well. After my relationship with Peter, I thought it would be impossible to trust someone again. But this man was different, so much so he undid my barriers. Also, unlike Peter's mother, Elian's family was full of life and happiness. There were no underlying hateful statements. Even the intense Lucia had warmed up to me. The way she harassed Elian made me smile. The two might not like to admit it, but anyone with eyes could see underneath their ongoing sibling rivalry was pure love and a great deal of attachment.

My ex's mother would never have touched me, much less kissed me on the mouth. I doubted there was enough alcohol on earth to make that happen. Again, just thinking of her sent shivers along my spine. I doubted I'd ever get over having that much venom thrown at me.

My mind started to slide down the slippery slope of self-doubt and skepticism when a middle-aged woman came up behind me and asked if she could share the area. Without waiting for an answer, she leaned against the post I was sitting on.

"Quite the party up there, huh?" she asked.

I smiled at the lady. "Yes, ma'am, it is a celebration."

"Do you know them?" she asked.

"Not really," I admitted. "I'm here with a date."

"Date not going so well?" she asked.

I smiled again. "No, it is going fine. Although, it has been a while since I've seen said date," I said with a chuckle. "I'm guessing with the free-flowing alcohol, he is asleep under a chair somewhere."

The woman chuckled, too. "So, you must really like this one to come to a family gathering like this," she commented.

I hadn't mentioned it was a family gathering, so I assumed the woman must be a guest of the party as well. "I didn't know it was a family affair, to be honest," I said. "I was just told it was going to be a party."

The woman laughed. "That doesn't surprise me, considering who your date is."

I glanced at her and said, "So, you are coming from the party as well, then."

She nodded her head. "I am... but like you, I sometimes need to get away. The family can be very intense. My name is Bonita Alverez. I think you met my husband Raul earlier today."

"You are Elian's aunt," I said with a little shock, rewinding what I'd said earlier, hoping I hadn't been offensive.

"Sí," she responded. "I saw you wander off after Lucia danced with you. I hope she didn't say something to offend you."

I laughed, "No, she seems to like me, which is good because I'm guessing she could be quite a handful if she didn't."

The older woman sighed deeply. "You have no idea. When you walked away, I was afraid. Lucia and Elian tend to battle each other, but she is fiercely protective of her brother and all of us, really. If she likes you, then you must be worth liking. She doesn't tend to allow many people in. We call her the family watchdog."

I nodded my understanding. "You would think Elian would avoid her, but he brought me to her restaurant on our first date, then told her I was a food critic. At first, I thought she was going to tackle me and rip me limb from limb."

Bonita laughed. "She could have, too. Never doubt that." She stared ponderingly at the ocean and said, "It is strange that he would bring you there, at least at first. He must have wanted to size you up. Lucia is the best judge of character. There is some inner compass in her that points toward good and bad. If she doesn't like someone, we've all learned to listen to her instincts. If she does, well, they tend to be okay. Our boy must have wanted to consider your measure."

I wasn't sure if I liked this or not. At first, I'd assumed I'd been brought to Lucia's to conduct a free review of her cooking. Then, I took Elian's word that he'd wanted to use his sister as a way to show me he wasn't just about the money, which of course, made me even more suspicious. However, it appeared the review Elian wanted wasn't *from* me, but *about* me.

"I guess since I'm here, I must have passed her compass test. Tonight, before I walked down here, she told me I was the perfect match for Elian."

The woman returned her attention back to me and asked, "This is what made you uncomfortable?"

"Not uncomfortable," I responded honestly. "I've just been burned by someone in the past. His mother was pretty tyrannical, and she said some really nasty stuff to me. When I told him, he turned on me. He and I had been engaged..."

I was surprised I'd disclosed so much to a stranger, and worse, a stranger who was related to a man who I was here with. "I'm sorry," I said, "I think I may have had too much to drink. I don't usually spill my guts to strangers on the beach."

"No worries, young man, I have that effect on people," she said, patting my arm.

"You need to know two things, which you won't believe right now. First, my nephew is a stand-up man. He is solid as a rock, and I know because I'm one of the people who raised him. You can—and I think eventually you will—trust him. Second, we are far from perfect, but when one of us finds that special someone, we will bring you into our family and love you as if you were always a part of it. That is just how we are made. I'm very sorry you were hurt in the past, but give this one a chance. You might be surprised by him."

She pushed away from the post, then laid her hand on mine. "I am headed back up to the party. You should come, too. I'm sure you have been missed by now." Then, she leaned over and kissed my cheek.

"I'll be back up in a moment. I would just like a little more time to process."

"You take all the time you need, querido. I'll let them know you are fine." She left me alone after that.

Things were moving too fast. Sure, it'd been a while since Peter and I split, but the pain from it was just as intense as it had been when it first happened. I wasn't ready for a serious relationship and I sure as hell wasn't ready to be meeting some man's very large and very involved family. If I had my car here, I'd have already left, but as it was, I was dependent on Elian. I liked this family, but it was time to put on the brakes. Time to protect my heart.

When I got back to the party, Elian was waiting for me. He looked at me, concerned. "Elian, thank you, for tonight, but I'm really not ready for this. I've already ordered a cab, so you don't have to leave your party."

I kissed Elian on the cheek and walked toward the stairs that led up to the front of the condominiums. "Can you tell me what we did wrong?" Elian asked.

This stopped me in my tracks. I turned around, worried that Elian had gotten the wrong impression.

"You did nothing wrong, none of you did. Your family is amazing, and I liked everyone I met, but Elian, I had a nasty breakup that I'm not over. I just wasn't ready for all this," I said as I gestured back toward the party. "I'm sorry, this was just too much." Then, all I could do was shake my head and walk away.

Elian called my name again, but I decided to keep walking. I was going to put an end to this, and as I walked away, I figured I had.

I was relieved when Elian hadn't tried to call me the next day. There was some regret, but having left things like I did, I probably had put an end to the whole mess.

I called Kristine first thing and told her what had happened the previous evening, with the goal of talking her into coming over to hang as I got stinking drunk.

She, of course, refused to do that, but she did say she'd be glad to take me out to get me hammered. "Just as a girlfriend should," she added.

She arrived at my apartment around seven in the evening and had a party of women with her, many of whom worked with us at the paper. "Tonight," Kristine said, "you need to party with girlfriends, no men allowed, and certainly no man's damned family."

I laughed and agreed. After Peter and I had broken up, my friendship with Janice, and my new relationship with Kristine, had pulled me through. Although, back then, there was a lot less getting hammered and a lot more eating ice cream. These friendships were just what I needed.

Unfortunately, this time I was the one who'd left the guy at the beach, literally and figuratively. It was better to end things before they became too intense, and having intimate discussions with a guy's aunt about becoming a member of their family was way too intense for a second date.

The men-trashing party was fully underway as we left my apartment. Kristine had ordered a limo to transport the group of us. This was perfect. As soon as I stepped into the limo, the beer and wine were passed around, and Kristine ordered me to fill the group in on what had happened.

When I explained that Elian had brought me to his sister's restaurant on a first date, all the women moaned in unison. "Oh, that isn't the worst of it," Kristine replied. "Tell them about your second date."

I shook my head. "It was his parents' anniversary party." Kristine yelled, "Anniversary party? His damned parents' anniversary party! Can you imagine?" The entire limo was full of women's voices, lifted in unison at the outrage.

"So, what did you do?" Renee, a woman I worked with but didn't know very well, asked.

I responded, "I danced. I got drunk. I kissed his mother on the lips, or actually, I got kissed on the lips by his mother. I got overwhelmed, and I ordered a cab and came home... where I've been licking my wounds ever since."

"The bastard," one of the other women said. "Who takes a first date to meet someone's family? No one," she answered her own question. "No one does that!"

"I liked them," I said too quietly, then turned toward the group. "I actually liked them. They were sweet and accommodating and even understanding but..." I drifted off, then said to the woman next to me, "Pass me another beer. I plan to get totally wasted, ladies."

They all cheered, but not as much as they had before. "Martin," Kristine asked, "if you liked them, why did you leave?"

After a moment I replied, "It isn't them, it was me. Actually, it was Peter, or at least his mother." Everyone seemed confused, except Kristine, who just looked sad.

I sighed then explained, "Peter is my ex. We were actually engaged to be married, at least for a few days. His mother was a psychopath who hated me. So, on Christmas Eve, she cornered me where Peter couldn't hear and ripped me up and down, saying some of the nastiest things anyone has ever said to me. When I told him what she said, he broke up with me, telling me it was best that he understood what kind of person I was before we got married."

Several of the women gasped. "Oh, honey," Renee said and put her hand on mine.

"So, last night, I'm at this party and hanging out with these people, and they were all wonderful, but I couldn't think of anything except that horrible woman. No amount of alcohol drowned out her hatred. So I ran. I'm a total chickenshit that ran away because I was being haunted by my ex's evil mother. How pathetic is that?" I asked the group.

"Not pathetic at all," Kenise, a woman I'd not met before tonight, said in a Jamaican accent. "There is nothing worse than a man's evil mother. My first husband's mother was Lucifer himself wrapped in the cloak of a woman's body. She terrorized me from the day we met until the day I cast her spawn aside. If anyone can haunt your dreams, Martin, it's the mother of your man."

The rest of the women agreed with her and each took turns sharing horrifying encounters with disapproving mothers. "We should all vow never to be evil mothers," Kristine chimed in, and they all toasted the vow.

The night was exactly what I needed. We drank, danced, bar-hopped, ogled men, and then trash-talked them in general when we got back into the limo. I got way past drunk, and I wasn't exactly sure when we got back home, but somehow, I'd been dumped back in my apartment and into my bed.

***

I woke the next morning to a monster hangover. Crawling out of bed, I was surprised I didn't upchuck the night's consumed liquor. Luckily, I managed to make it to the kitchen where I whipped up my hangover treatment, downed it, gagged, and lay back down on my sofa until the room stopped spinning.

The door buzzer echoed in my head. Assuming it was Kristine come back to check on me, I stood only long enough to buzz her in, then lay back on the sofa, covering my eyes with the pillow.

I heard the door open and shut. "How can you be awake after all we drank last night?" I asked.

Then, I heard, "*Ahem*, Martin. It is me, Elian."

Without taking the pillow off my face, I replied, "Shit, Elian. Why are you here?"

"I came to apologize. Were you expecting someone else?" he asked.

"No, not really, but I assumed you were Kristine come to harass me about my hangover."

I slowly removed the pillow from my eyes and slanted them at Elian. "You didn't need to come. I was an ass and left you hanging. It should be me who's apologizing. It just took ten gallons of assorted varieties of alcohol to figure that out."

Elian smiled. "If you stick to just one type of drink per night, the hangover isn't quite a bad the next day. A trick my papa taught me when I turned twenty-one."

"Yes," I replied, "but your papa wasn't hanging out with a group of men-hating, vengeful women last night. We were all plying ourselves with alcohol to nurse our men-inspired wounds."

"You needed to apply ten gallons of alcohol to nurse wounds I created?" I could hear the hurt in his voice.

"No, silly," I replied. "I haven't known you long enough to get that many wounds from you. These were wounds created before I moved to Fort Lauderdale."

Elian

I watched him as he got out two Alka-Seltzers from the cabinet and dropped them into a small glass of water. When the fizz died down, he downed the drink in one gulp. Then, he leaned over the counter, waiting for his stomach to settle. He sighed, then turned back to me.

"You don't know me well, Elian. I probably should have been more upfront with you, but, honestly, I didn't think you'd expose me to your family this early in the game. We haven't even decided if we like each other or not. Hell, before the kiss I gave you in front of your uncle, who, by the way, I didn't know was there, we hadn't even kissed. At least not a real kiss. For all I know, you didn't even think I was attractive. Most of the time, my dates and I would have had sex twice and secretly vowed never to see each other again at this point. That's the usual lifespan of my post–Peter, my ex," I clarified, "dates."

Before I could speak, Martin turned green. "Hold that thought," he said and rushed to his bathroom.

"Wow," Martin said when he returned, "I must have drunk more last night than I usually do. I don't usually puke after step two."

"Lie back down," I said. "I have something that will help. Can I use your kitchen?"

Martin moaned but lay down. "Be my guest," he whimpered.

A few minutes later, I came in with a damp washcloth and a concoction that my sister taught me after a bender I went on when I was twenty-one and new to the drinking scene, well at least newly legal. It smelled almost as bad as it looked, but it worked like a charm.

"I am not going to drink that," Martin said.

"You will if you want to feel better," I countered.

Martin stared at me as he sat back up. He held his nose and swallowed the drink. "Oh, that's nasty," he said and lay back down.

I opened the wet washcloth full size and laid the entire thing over Martin's face. "Let that sit there until you begin feeling better," I said, then leaned back against the coffee table while Martin lay motionless on the sofa.

Within a few minutes, Martin asked, "What did you put in that?"

"It is a family secret," I responded with a chuckle, thinking my sister would be proud of me for pretending like it was a state secret.

"The secret is you use it before abuela comes in and finds out you have a hangover." I chuckled at the old family joke. "I'll write down the recipe. You can make it beforehand and have it in the fridge when you know you are going out drinking. I learned long ago that it is always good to be prepared."

"Mmm," was Martin's response as he continued to lie still with the cloth over his face.

"Tell me again why you are here, Elian," Martin asked without moving.

"I'm here because my mother and aunt demanded that I come. They were both pretty angry when they found out you'd left. Mi tía told Mama that you had a bad experience with your ex's family, so it was come here and apologize or be disowned."

Without taking the washcloth off his face, he signed the cross in the air, and said, "You are forgiven. Now go and sin no more."

I couldn't help but chuckle. "I was wrong, Martin. I shouldn't have thrown you to the lions, literally the lion, Lucia, and I should have asked if you minded going to the anniversary party instead of just springing it on you."

Martin took the washcloth off his face and asked, "Yeah, why did you do that?"

"I like you," I replied.

"If you liked me," Martin said, "then you should've communicated better."

I nodded and said, "As I've been told by every female in my family, as well as my uncle. They all like you, more than I'd expected, really."

"Yeah, that doesn't help your case, Elian," he said.

"No, I can see that now. My family is very important to me, Martin. I've dated quite a bit, and I've never had a man I wanted to know as much as I have you. You are funny, no-nonsense, and hold me to a higher standard than most men. I just thought it'd be nice to introduce you to my loved ones and see what they thought of you—to see if their instinct was the same as mine. I was right, and they agree with me, but my tactics might have been a bit misguided."

"Ya think?" Martin replied.

"I want to make it up to you, Martin. Can I take you on a real date? No family involved."

"No," Martin said, matter-of-fact. "I'm not in any condition to date, not seriously, and if we date, I can already see it will be serious—too damned serious!"

I nodded. "I thought you'd say that, so I have another proposition."

I could tell the headache was beginning to wane because he sat up waiting for my response.

"I need to explore restaurants in the entertainment district to invest in, and you need to do reviews. I propose we use this to our mutual advantage."

Martin squinted his eyes; I could tell he was waiting for the other shoe to drop. "We are both looking for the same things," I continued. "Great service, style, food quality, and taste. If we team up, we can get through more of them quicker, and it will be more fun doing it as a team."

Martin put the cloth back over his eyes, but I could tell he was thinking about my proposal. "It always pays to have someone with you when you go to review a restaurant, bar, or other venues. When you go alone, it either says you are seeking a date or that you are a food critic. This could work, but there will be clear boundaries if I agree."

I laughed. "Martin, I would expect nothing less from you."

Lifting the corner of the cloth, he peered at me and asked, "Are you willing to hear my conditions?"

"Absolutely," I replied. "What are your commands, General?"

"General," Martin repeated. "You think you're cute."

He replaced the cloth and began. "Number one: These are not dates, and will never be dates. You can't call them dates, and you can't use them to get into my pants. These are strictly professional meetings where we will *pretend* to be on dates to evaluate the quality of the restaurants, bars, and venues. Do you agree to number one?"

I hesitated. "So, if we decide to go on a date, it will be different from these?" I waited for a reaction, and when I didn't get one, I accepted it, shrugging. "I agree."

"Number two: We agree not to date. This is strictly a professional relationship, and we will both agree not to mingle romance with business." I was about to argue with him, considering the whole thing was so I could have another chance with him, but when I opened my mouth, Martin chimed in. "This one is non-negotiable. It's a take it or leave it thing. Do you agree?"

Apparently having no choice, I begrudgingly said, "I think it is unfair that you won't consider dating me, but if this is the only way, I agree. However, I want it on the record that I'm agreeing under duress."

Martin chuckled. "Record noted.

"Number three: If anyone asks if we are dating, the answer is 'sort of.' It will get out fairly quickly that we are teamed up to write reviews, unless the community thinks we are genuinely dating. That means you have to date when you are either out of town or somewhere it won't get out that we aren't together."

"That is no problem with me," I replied. "I rarely date someone when I'm seeking to invest in an area. Creates too much unnecessary drama."

"Number four: You must be absolutely upfront and honest with your family about the arrangement. They *cannot* be left to imagine there is more to us than this business arrangement. I can already tell your family is like mine. Once they get something in their minds, they are relentless. If you give them even a tiny shred of hope, they will be tenacious. Correct?"

"Yes, you are correct," I replied.

"Do you agree to sit them down and lay the rules out about our relationship, including this one?" Martin asked.

"I do."

"Finally, and the most important, number five: If you decide to purchase a business inside my critique area, you will agree to give me three full months to publicly break up with you before you close."

I thought for a moment. "That is probably okay, except, sometimes, I come across a business that is going to fail if not rescued. If I get one of those, I will tell you immediately, and we can have an official breakup before I sign the contract. That is all I can promise," I replied.

"I think that'll work. We just have to ensure there is no one thinking I'm playing favorites for you.

"That's it," Martin said. "Those are my requirements for participation."

"Okay," I agreed, then let my evil smile take over. "First mission is this morning. I have a little bistro down on the riverwalk that I need to check out."

"Today?" Martin asked.

"Yep, today," I responded.

"No, not on hangover Sunday. Let's start tomorrow."

"Nope, can't do it. I'm headed to Dallas tomorrow, but I'm available right now."

Martin gave me a nasty look and accused me of being a sadist.

"Maybe a little," I said, "but you'll feel better in a moment. "

"I already feel better, but not necessarily 'go out in public' better."

"We can assume that some of your readers will be going to this bistro hungover, so isn't this a perfect opportunity for you to assess whether or not this is a good place for that kind of follow-up activity?"

Martin just stared at me blankly, totally uninspired by my hangover assessment idea.

After we stared at each other for several minutes, Martin said, "I need a shower and to get dressed. I'm planning to take my time, and you'll just have to hang out."

"Fine," I agreed. "I'll just sit here and admire your apartment. Take your time."

My sarcasm earned another hateful look from him, but I could tell he wasn't in the mood to argue any longer.

Martin didn't hurry through the shower or dressing. I assumed he was exerting a bit of passive-aggressive revenge on me for forcing him to get ready.

I went outside to call the bistro to ensure we had a table. They tended to be packed on Sunday mornings after ten o'clock, and if Martin's "slow to get ready" behavior was any indication, it was going to be closer to eleven before we got there.

When I walked back in the door, Martin was coming out of his kitchen. "Oh, hi. Finally dressed I see."

"Yeah," Martin replied. "I thought maybe you gave up and left."

"No such luck," I replied.

"I decided to give the owner of the bistro a call and let him know I'm coming down this morning. I didn't, however, tell him I was bringing a food critic. This should be fun."

Martin gave me another one of his hateful looks, then said, "You are, under no circumstances, to tell him that I am one. This morning, I am only a dude going out for some food that will hopefully cut down on the headache that seems to get bigger the longer I talk to you."

I laughed at Martin's comment. "All in a day's work." Then, I took him by the hand and led him out of the apartment. "You can ride with me. That way, the old man who owns the bistro will think you are just some arm candy I brought with me."

"Yeah, arm candy..." Martin replied dryly.

As we cruised along in my car, once again speeding along together, I talked about my frustrations with my new business acquisition in Dallas. "I don't really know what is causing the place to struggle. It is in a nice location. The staff that caused problems before have all been replaced. We serve tasty food, but our sales continue to stagnate."

"What type of food do you serve?" Martin asked.

"Mexican American... basically Tex-Mex," I replied.

"Where is the restaurant again?"

"Downtown."

"Is that close to the arts district?" Martin asked.

"Yes, right in the middle of it, actually."

"I think I know your problem. You are competing with Los Pecos. That is where everyone goes to party, drink, eat Tex-Mex, et cetera. They have been there for over fifty years. What is your price range?" he asked.

"Our prices are less than Los Pecos. The former owner's goal was to undercut them and draw the night crowd with cheaper drinks," I replied while massaging my forehead. "It should be a foolproof plan."

"I think you are thinking about this backward. Los Pecos is a rustic, everyday eating place, and although a bit pricey, they are still affordable enough that they remain the most popular venue in town." Martin lay his head back against the headrest but continued to talk. "There are several other Mexican restaurants using the same tactic, but what the arts district lacks is a before- and after-meal meeting place. If you could retrofit your restaurant so people could either start the night there with drinks or after for dessert, you could probably make more money off those items than you do your main menu. In fact, every time I've been in Dallas with friends, they've wanted a place to go after a movie or even after we ate. The problem is the only place that focuses on that is the Dessert Factory, and the line to get into there is at least an hour long, even on Sunday and Monday nights. Unfortunately, if you take my advice, your desserts will have to be as good, if not better, than Dessert Factory."

I turned to Martin, who still had his head back and eyes closed. "Are you sure you aren't a businessman?"

Martin laughed. "No, if I had to be a businessman, I'd be out of business. I just like to eat. It is my job to know when there is something lacking, restaurant-wise, and when someone works to fill the void. If you'd read my column, you'd know I often take note, and even comment on these needs in the paper's blog. There is definitely a void there, and you could easily fill it if you are creative."

"I think I'm going to like this arrangement," I said.

"Good," Martin responded. "Brunch is on you then."

I looked back at Martin and, in a voice I'm sure reflected my surprise, asked, "I thought you had an expense account?"

"Ha, not in this part of town," Martin replied. "Oh, rich boy, this has to be an addendum to our arrangement. Consider this my number six. When not in the area of town I'm assigned, the food is on you."

I laughed again but didn't argue. Martin didn't seem to care, though; he probably already knew he could get me to comply.

Although I knew I was good at business, I also knew business people more often than not missed the important elements of the restaurant business that only a consumer could point out to us. I knew Martin would be a valuable asset. So, there was no reason why I couldn't be a good asset for him as well.

When we arrived at the bistro, it was a quarter past eleven. It appeared to have a good Sunday following. The server kindly took our name and informed us it would be about an hour wait. The crowd outside was younger and appeared to be the morning after-party crowd.

"Looks like you are in with the right people," I teased. "You're clearly not the only person here with a hangover."

Several people around us heard me and their snickering, as well as a few green-tinted faces, confirmed my suspicions.

Within seconds of our arrival, my friend came out to meet us. "Senor. Whitman," the man said, "thank you for coming to our Sunday brunch."

"It is our pleasure, señor Hernandez," I said.

The older man smiled, and then gestured toward the door. "Come with me. I'll show you to your table." I smiled at Martin, and we both followed the man into the bistro.

There were more than a few hateful looks as we walked past the half hungover crowd. When we got out of earshot, Martin whispered, "I'm used to being pulled to the front of the line, but you never get used to the angry looks of hungry patrons who you've jumped in front of."

The table we were shown to was in the back of the dining room and next to the kitchen door. You could see everything in the dining room from this vantage point. When we sat down, the older man sat with us. "Senor. Whitman..."

"Elian, please," I interrupted. "You have known me since before I was born."

Señor Hernandez didn't even pause. "Sí, pero esto es un negocio, siempre use el titulo de un hombre cuando esta hacienda negocios." Then, the older man turned to Martin and asked, "Don't you agree, señor, it is better to use a title when you are doing business?"

Martin smiled. "I grew up in Texas, señor. I was taught you always use a person's title, along with 'yes, ma'am' and 'yes, sir,' when addressing anyone older than you."

Señor Hernandez smiled back, and then turned to me and said, "This one is very smart and has been raised well.

"So, senor. Whitman, you want to buy my bistro, sí?"

I shook my head and honestly replied, "No, I've not made up my mind, señor. I am here to eat first, get to know your business, and see if it needs me or if some other buyer may be more appropriate."

"I see," he said. "Your papa said you were wanting to buy businesses in the area now that you sold your brewery."

"He told you the truth, señor, but again, I only wish to buy a business that I can improve. It appears to me you have already made the place perfect."

The gentleman stared at me for a moment, then smiled and slapped me on the back. "You have the charm of your mama, but you are as sneaky as your uncle. I can see I will get nowhere this way. So, I will let my food and servers convince you."

Rising, he said, "Enjoy yourselves. I will send you the house specials." He disappeared into the back and in an extraordinarily short time, the food began to arrive. Plates and plates of it, to the point he brought a table from the back to put the overflow on.

The other customers, who had given us hateful looks when we were given a table in front of them, now looked at us with wonder.

We ate more than we should have, and the food was nice; not top of the line but definitely nice. Martin and I had a pleasant conversation about how the area had changed over the past couple of years and how older venues like this one were getting a new life. We talked about Miami and how Fort Lauderdale was so much easier to live in, both agreeing it was because there was less traffic and less tourist chaos.

We both agreed we liked Miami, though, and I promised to take Martin to a couple of my favorite restaurants there. "I promise you, you haven't heard of these because they are not for tourists, and no one there speaks English. The food is magnificent."

Martin reminded me that our agreement was for Fort Lauderdale, but said he might let a couple of extra-special restaurants slide through if I promised they were over-the-top good, like on the same level of my sister Lucia's restaurant.

When we were done, the servers collected all the plates, and without requesting it, they brought out three large doggie bags of leftover food. Señor Hernandez came out and sat with us again.

I could tell Martin was afraid he was about to be grilled about the food, as I assumed was the case when a restaurant owner found out he was a critic, but señor Hernandez didn't push for compliments. Instead, he said, "I hope you enjoyed the food. Senor, your papa probably told you, it's time for me to sell.

"I recently had a cancer removed from my lung, and my doctors tell me I'm cured, but there is nothing like cancer to wake you up. I'm going to sell out and spend more time with my family. You know, I have been so busy here that I haven't had time to go back to Cuba, even though they opened the borders. I need to go see my mama while she's still living."

I put my hand on the man's shoulder and said, "I will see what I can do, señor. I will be back in touch by the end of the week."

We all stood, shook hands, then Martin and I left with the doggie bags. As we walked back to my car, I asked Martin what he thought of the food.

"It was mediocre but not bad."

"What were your thoughts about the prices?" I asked.

Martin laughed. "I like free."

I poked him in the ribs, as if to say, "you know what I mean."

"I thought the prices were reasonable, maybe a bit too low for the area. There could be a ten percent increase, and the cost would still be about ten percent less than the rest of the restaurants in the area."

"If you were going to give the restaurant a review, what would you say?" I persisted.

"I'd have to do the tallies, but I'm guessing I'd give the old building a four out of five. It was immaculately clean but a bit run-down and in need of updating. Food, I think, gets a four, but mainly because it was hot and tasted okay. Service would easily get a four-point-five, but I'd want to see it when they aren't expecting us. I'm guessing when señor Hernandez isn't there the service isn't quite as attentive."

"Which explains why he hasn't made it back to Cuba to see his mama," I sighed.

"Exactly," Martin agreed. "If I were you, I would be concerned about how well it would function when you aren't there."

"I'm not going to buy it," I admitted. "I do know someone who might. Yes, I agree the only way this works is if the person who takes it over from señor Hernandez wants to run the place in a similar way."

We continued to chat about the restaurant: who would be the best buyer, and some small, inexpensive ways the place could be improved to support the existing crowd and ensure it survived for the foreseeable future.

As we pulled up in front of Martin's apartment building, I asked him, "How is your headache?"

He hesitated, then smiled. "It's gone. I guess eating a Thanksgiving meal for brunch is just the cure for a hangover."

I chuckled. "That, and abuela's secret hangover recipe."

"You should bottle that," Martin said.

I came around the car and waited for Martin to get out. I was seriously thinking about kissing him, but Martin quickly put his hand out to shake mine. "It was fun, and I appreciate you getting me out. I would have probably stayed in and stared at my bedroom ceiling if you hadn't."

I accepted his handshake with a smile. "I am happy we are going to work together. You have some valuable insight, Martin."

With that, Martin turned toward his apartment building but quickly turned back around and asked, "When are you back in town?"

"Next week," I replied. "I think I'll be back Monday of next week."

"Perfect," Martin replied. "You owe me dinner at a new Italian place that just opened up in my district. I'll email you what nights I'm free. Don't wear white. I hear it is messy."

I stood for a moment, smiling after he disappeared into his building. I let out a sigh and said to the closed door, "I am not done courting you, Martin Williams. You are too special to let go that easily." I climbed back into my car and sped off back toward the beach and the condo that, at this time on a Sunday afternoon, would be bursting at the seams with family.

Martin

The following week, Elian met me at the little family-owned Italian restaurant that had just opened next to the Riverwalk Fort Lauderdale. The family had another restaurant in Kansas City, but the granddaughter of the KC restaurant owners decided to move to this area and was hell-bent on creating the same quality restaurant that had endured for two generations in her hometown.

We walked into the restaurant and the atmosphere immediately impressed me. The seating flowed nicely in a well-designed space. Candles flickered on tables, adding to the ambiance created by low lighting and old-style Italian music that blended classic arias with just the right smattering of Old Blue Eyes, played at the perfect level for conversation.

There was a short wait I thought must be due to its newness. A small, intimate venue like this one would have a strong following soon. I guessed the older crowd would especially love the atmosphere. When we were seated, the host told us they had a pasta bar tonight and gave a menu of ingredients for the bar, along with the regular menus. She disappeared and returned a moment later with waters in each hand.

I excused myself and got up, using my typical pretense of the restroom as a way to inspect the restaurant without being conspicuous. I spotted the pasta bar tucked next to the alcohol bar and grinned at the ingenuity. From the crowd of people around the pasta bar, I had to assume some of them would decide to grab a drink while they waited for the chef to cook their food. In fact, I noticed several people standing in the bar area with drinks who appeared to be doing just that.

I returned to the table as a server appeared and brought with her a nice loaf of scrumptious-smelling bread. She asked what drinks we'd like. Elian ordered one, but I decided I wanted to see how the bartender handled what could very likely be a bottleneck from the folks coming to the pasta bar.

I convinced Elian to order something from the menu and asked him to ply the server a lot of questions to try to put her off her game. "I want to see how well the new servers handle a high maintenance customer."

Elian smiled and said, "I am good at being high maintenance." I'd been all business and sort of forgot Elian was there as a bystander. His teasing brought me back to reality. I smiled and said, "I really do appreciate you coming with me. It helps to appear to be on a date."

"No problem," Elian replied. "I like playing the role."

The server returned with Elian's drink and asked to take our order. As requested, Elian pored over the menu, acting as if he was indecisive. The young woman smiled patiently, and answered a couple of his questions, which he turned into more questions. Nothing seemed to cause her to falter.

"Can you tell me what sounds good?" she finally asked.

"I don't know, something Italian," Elian said with absolutely no indication that he was joking.

"Well, that is very easy," she said with a smile. "When I'm hungry for something hearty, I usually go for a white sauce. The mixture of cream and pasta tends to fill me up, but when I want just traditional, delicious Italian, I go for the red sauces. Of course, if you are really wanting to save room for dessert, the soup and salad are quite nice. The soup tonight is minestrone. It is my grandmama's own secret recipe that I talked her out of before coming to Fort Lauderdale," she said.

I caught the "grandmother"comment and quickly asked, "Are you the owner here?"

The woman smiled and answered, "Yes, I am serving tonight to help my new staff get their sea legs under them before they take over."

"It's lovely that you are taking such a personal interest," Elian said. "I grew up with a family that insisted we all be personally involved with the business. You could say that is in my blood."

Just then, a customer called for her. She turned and said, "Excuse me. I'll be right back."

The lady who had called her seemed to be upset about something. I leaned closer to the edge to hear. "This drink has too much alcohol in it," the woman said.

The young owner was pleasant and said, "Oh, dear, I'll take that back and have them fix that for you right away. This is a martini, correct?"

"That is correct, dear, thank you," the woman said and turned back to her conversation. The server took the drink to the bar and returned promptly to their table. As she spoke, the bartender himself brought the corrected martini to the woman and waited for her to take a sip. When she smiled, the bartender left and returned to his place behind the bar.

Elian ordered the minestrone soup and the eggplant parmesan. I went to the pasta bar, which had three people in front of me. The chef seemed to be well prepared, though, and it only took a few minutes for the other customers' food to be cooking as he turned his attention on me.

"Can you tell me what sauces you have here?" I asked. The chef had all the trimmings: the white outfit, the hat, and just the right amount of foodie attitude.

"Of course," the man said with a slight Italian accent. "The three red sauces are all homemade. You have a traditional beef marinara, an onion–basil and garlic gazpacho, and a bacon marinara with red pepper flakes. That one is rather spicy. The white sauce choices are basic alfredo or a wine and lemon cream sauce."

Then I played dumb, asking about the noodles and other ingredients. I had intentionally asked these questions to see if it would interrupt the chef's routine, and I wanted to see if I could mix the man up. However, it didn't. The chef answered my questions with respect and expediency, all the while serving up the food to previous customers.

Finally, I made my mind up and paired white wine and lemon cream sauce with fettuccine and chicken with chopped bacon on top. While the food cooked, I slipped over to the bar and ordered a drink I hadn't seen on the menu. The bartender smiled. "I like the Moscow Mule myself. I'm afraid we don't have copper cups here, though. Is it okay for me to put it in a regular glass for you?"

"That'll be just fine," I replied. I was impressed by the bartender's ability to negotiate with me, giving me what I wanted, but also ensuring I understood that the traditional copper cup wasn't an option. I considered being upset about the lack of copper cups, but I'd already seen how the bartender had managed the upset woman and decided to give him a break. Besides, my pasta order was done, and it smelled absolutely amazing.

When I got back to the table with both my drink and the pasta, Elian smiled at me. "You've been busy," he commented.

"I guess so. Where is all the bread?" I asked.

Elian winked at me. "Sorry," he replied, and the apology was far from genuine. "That bread was truly out of this world. I thought we should give you a chance to ask for more, just to see the reaction." Then, he gave me a sly smile that reminded me of a little boy who had just taken one of his mother's cookies while she was still letting them cool.

"You are naughty young man," I teased. When I was about to ask for another loaf, the owner came out with a customer's order. She dropped it off and turned to us with another loaf. She placed this one next to me, and winking at Elian, said, "I thought this might keep the conversation civil over here."

Elian laughed in spite of himself. When she was gone, he said, "I like her. I'd try to convince her to join one of my ventures if I were still in the business here and she didn't own this one."

"Yeah, I like her, too. She knows what she is doing," I replied.

The rest of the night went splendidly. The food was on par with the service, and the other customers all seemed to be enjoying themselves. Even the other wait staff seemed happy and competent. When we were done with our meal, the owner came out with two pieces of rum cake and placed them in front of us.

"We didn't order these," I said.

The lady chuckled. "It comes with the meal. My grandmama demands that every customer leaves with something sweet on their tongue. It is supposed to remind you how much we care here at Cara Vetchies."

She winked at us and asked if she could bring us anything else.

"One moment," I said. I took a bite and rolled my eyes in delight. "I think I love your grandmama."

The server laughed at me. I added, "I will have a decaffeinated coffee, *if* that's available."

"Yes, we do. It'll take a moment because we brew our decaffeinated fresh for each customer. Is that okay?"

"Yes, of course," I replied.

Our server dashed off to get the coffee started. I put my cake aside while waiting and was surprised at how fast the woman returned with my cup. "I thought you had to make this fresh," I said.

"We do," the server agreed. "We make our own K-cups with our family's coffee brand." She seemed to be waiting for me to taste the coffee and add the cream.

I tasted it and smiled at her. "This is good for decaffeinated. What is your family's brand?" I asked.

"It's one we have been improving on many years. It's from Peru but roasted in Kansas City at the little roastery there. When you are leaving, you can stop by the bar. The bags of coffee are there." She smiled again and left us to our dessert and my coffee.

"This is really impressive," I said to Elian. "If I were going to buy a place, this would be it."

"And why is that?" Elian asked.

I put my finger to my chin, acting like I knew what I was talking about. "Clearly, this is a spin-off of another restaurant, so it has the franchise potential, but there have definitely been some improvements here that are likely not what is done in Kansas City. Modernization without jeopardizing the integrity of the food."

"You have a good eye," Elian said. "I was thinking the same thing, but I will wait to see how she does a year from now. If she is able to maintain the quality, I may ask her to consider a partnership with me. I doubt it would be able to be successful without the family's involvement, though, and trust me, I know better than most that family isn't always interested in the long-term business potential." Then, Elian laughed, knowing I knew he was talking about his sister.

When the owner returned with our check, both Elian and I congratulated her on the restaurant and ensured her that this was one of the best food experiences we'd had in a long time. The young restaurateur smiled from ear to ear.

"Please tell others," she said. "It takes good word of mouth to get a new restaurant off the ground."

"No doubt," I agreed. "I promise we will share our experiences with anyone who will listen." I could tell the young woman thought I was talking about telling my friends. She would be surprised to learn I was a critic, and I'd be telling the general public about this wonderful little restaurant. I couldn't help but hope she was ready for the onslaught of business that was about to hit her.

We walked out of the restaurant happy, full, and glad to have had such a great experience. "I believe this is going to become one of my places to come to when I want to wind down and not write a critique," I said.

"I have no doubt. I'll be coming back as well," Elian agreed.

As we walked to our cars, Elian leaned over and gave me a very civil kiss on the cheek. "See ya soon," he said. "I like our new arrangement. I can enjoy an evening with you and not have to worry about seducing you afterward. Maybe I need to develop more of these platonic relationships."

I involuntarily raised my eyebrow but didn't pursue the conversation. *Was Elian trying to make me jealous?*

Did it make me jealous? Maybe it did. This wasn't going to work if Elian ran around with several different men. If he was going to make the Fort Lauderdale restaurant world think we were only on a date, then he needed to play a monogamous part. "Let's talk about that later. In fact, meet me tomorrow for coffee. Should I come down to the beach?" I asked.

"No, I have a meeting downtown," Elian replied. "I can meet you somewhere near there at eight a.m. My meeting isn't until later. Does that work?"

"Sure, then let's meet at Crowsters next to my office building. You can park in the office parking lot and I'll comp your ticket."

I left before Elian could put another kiss on my cheek. I was sure this was probably just a European gesture Elian had adopted, but electrical currents coursed through me even when he barely touched me. His kiss short-circuited my brain. Oh, and he smelled so amazing. That in and of itself made my head swim. No, I couldn't let him kiss me again or I would lose all control. I was determined not to let that happen. Not when I had so much to lose.

Elian

The next morning, I was at the coffee shop before Martin arrived. I'd texted him to get his coffee order and had it waiting when he arrived.

"You are up early," Martin said when he came in.

"I was excited to see you," I replied.

I could tell I'd knocked him off his guard. "That's good, I suppose," he replied.

I'd chosen a spot at the counter overlooking the street because of how close the two seats were. When Martin sat down, I could smell the soap on him. I also caught a faint whiff of what must be aftershave or cologne, which was very subtle and extremely sexy. I liked the way his short cropped brown hair fell over his forehead, making him appear a bit younger than he was.

"So, what is next on our restaurant agenda?" Martin asked.

"I have to be out of town again next week," I replied. "In fact, I wanted to ask if you'd be willing to fly out to Dallas this weekend for a little moonlighting." Martin looked at me skeptically, almost like he could bolt out the door at any moment.

I quickly added, "I'd like for you to critique my restaurant and give me some clues on how to make it more like what you recommended."

I could tell he was taken aback.

"You know I'm not a businessman, Elian. I just know food."

"You know a lot more than you think," I replied. "But if it makes you feel better, it is the food that we are in the business of selling. Being able to find the right mix of good food, good service, and a happy atmosphere are the three ingredients to a successful food business. Correct?"

Martin agreed. "Well, what's in it for me, Mr. Whitman?" he teased.

I smiled, knowing I'd at least intrigued the guy. "Two things," I replied. "First, a free trip to Dallas, all expenses paid. And second, you get to spend some time in my valuable company."

Martin choked on his coffee before he responded. "You are sure of yourself, huh?"

"Oh," I added, "I also pay about seventy-five dollars per hour for a consulting fee. I think you'll find that is the industry standard."

Martin slowly raised his left eyebrow. "You are willing to pay me that much to review your restaurant?"

"Yep," I responded without hesitation.

"Okay, no, I won't take your money, but if you will pay for my flight, a rental car, and provide a good place to spend the night, I'm game. You can take me out to eat at fancy restaurants instead of paying me to be there."

"Whatever you wish," I replied. "If you do this for me, I can also pass your name around, and you will for sure get calls from restauranteurs across the nation. You have no idea what the need is for someone who can offer the types of strategic suggestions you seem to think of naturally."

Martin ignored my compliment and potential business offerings. I could see the internal war regarding whether he'd like doing that kind of consulting work or not. I knew he generally loved doing what he did for the customer and less for the business side of things.

Instead of responding, he redirected the conversation by saying, "One more thing: I will not spare your feelings with what I see. If it is a mess, I'll tell you straight up."

"That's what I'm hoping for," I replied.

We planned the trip, which took up most of the rest of our coffee date, and I left for my meeting feeling like I'd managed to accomplish a big part of my agenda to woo Martin.

Martin

I went into Kristine's office, sat down, and asked, "So, does it conflict with my contract to do consulting work outside of the city?"

Kristine shrugged. "I doubt it, but why?"

"Because Elian just asked me to go to Dallas for the weekend to consult about his restaurant there. He offered to pay me a ridiculous amount of money to do it, which I turned down, of course."

"You turned down a weekend with the Cuban prince?" she asked with a sneer.

"No, I turned down the money but made him agree to pay all the expenses."

"I seriously doubt it is a problem. A lot of our reporters moonlight, but if it makes you feel better, I'll send the question up to legal to find out for sure."

"I'd appreciate that," I said, then turned to leave.

Before I could go, Kristine asked, "So, is this going somewhere... the two of you?"

"No, I have the brakes fairly well secured, but I admit, he is beginning to get past my defenses. God, he smells like heaven, Kristine! But seriously, I'm in no way ready to be in a relationship, especially with a guy who throws a date into the deep end of meeting his family pool! All I can think of is the witch mother of my ex. I am not ready to take on another momzilla anytime soon."

"You didn't make it sound like his mom was a momzilla when we were out the other night. Do you think she is?" she asked.

"I didn't spend enough time with her to know," I replied honestly. "What I did have enough time to know is they are tight and would stick together against an outsider. I'm an outsider and one who is still nursing his wounds from the relationship war I lost."

Kristine came around the desk and leaned on the edge just across from me. "Honey, I know that had to have been bad, but eventually, you have to give people a chance to be better than the ones who hurt you. You are a marrying kind of guy. You aren't going to be fully happy until you have that husband, two kids, and the picket fence, wrapping you up neatly."

I gave Kristine a curious look. "You don't paint me in a very exciting light," I said.

"Just because you don't think domesticity is exciting doesn't mean it isn't what you crave. Don't feel bad. Most girls want the same thing." Then, she winked at me.

Later that afternoon, Kristine came to my office and relayed that legal said as long as I didn't moonlight in any of the restaurants I am reviewing or could potentially review for the paper, I was free to consult for them. "The paralegal said the attorney thought you should consult outside of the Fort Lauderdale area just to be safe."

"Cool," I replied.

"What's up?" Kristine asked.

"Well, you got my mind all messed up, Kristine. I'd convinced myself I was happy being alone. Now, you brought the truth up and threw it in my face. What the hell am I supposed to do with the truth?"

Kristine smiled. "You were just fooling yourself, Martin," she said. "The good news is, you don't have to get married today, but you really should give the man a chance before you kick him to the curb."

"I'll think about it," I said.

"Want a hug?" Kristine asked.

I nodded, feeling glad my boss was also my friend. Kristine hugged me and told me to hold my chin up. "If things crash and burn, I'll be there for you, and it isn't like I haven't become an expert on stupid breakups."

I laughed as I remembered nursing her through a couple of the latest ones.

"Okay, I'll think about it," I said again. "Maybe I'll test the waters this weekend and see what comes of it."

Kristine wagged her eyebrows and said, "I hope *someone* comes," and walked out the door.

I laughed at her silliness. I'd been damned lucky with my friendships with Janice and now Kristine. Two women who had made life richer and more fun. I knew I needed to set up a time for the two to meet each other officially. They'd seen each other two years ago when Janice had pulled me to a New Year's Eve party to help me get past my Peter breakup misery, but not since then.

I knew they would either hit it off or hate each other. The latter, a very likely possibility, being why I hadn't put them together before now.

Thinking of Janice, I texted her that I was going to Dallas this weekend to hang out with the guy I'd already told her about. "Can you come to meet me while I'm there?" I asked. "I'm going to review a restaurant, and I need a date."

"You want me to drive three hours to be your date to a work event?" she asked.

"Yep, pretty much," I responded, "and to spend time with me. You can spend the night with me at the hotel."

"Okay, I can come Friday night, but I have to leave the next day," she texted back. "I have a hot date Saturday night with the sexy redhead again... Oh, and I get the bed."

"We'll share the bed. How about that?"

"Do I get to sleep with the sexy Cuban?" she asked.

"No, he has to stay in a different room," I responded with a smiley face.

When she forced me to send a picture of him, she quickly replied, "He is too damned hot not to share a room with you *or* me! You are no fun!"

"Okay, I'll see you Friday night."

"Okay," was her final response.

Then I texted Elian. "My girlfriend from Austin is going to drive up Friday and join me. We can do the restaurant critique that night. She can stay in my hotel room, so no need to book another room for her."

Elian texted me back. "That sounds perfect. I can't be there until Saturday anyway. I'll book your ticket and give you directions on how to get into my apartment above the restaurant. You can stay with me if that is okay."

I wrote back, "Won't your staff see me coming out of your apartment? If they know we are friends, it could possibly corrupt the critique."

Elian responded, "No, there are three apartments, all occupied. They will probably just assume you are staying with one of the other residents."

I was not too sure how I felt about staying in Elian's apartment. When Janice left, that meant I'd be alone with him. I decided to text him back. "How many bedrooms does your apartment have?"

Elian texted back. "Three, but I use the third bedroom as my office. I can put an air mattress in there for your friend, though.

"That's fine," I replied, but not without some trepidation. Did I have the willpower to spend the night with him? *Of course, I did,* I tried to convince myself. *I'm not a horny teenager, and I'd put really good boundaries down. I just needed to stick with those and all would be fine.*

The rest of the week went by fast, and I was becoming more and more excited about the weekend. I was desperate to hang with Janice again. I was also curious about what Elian had done with his new restaurant in Dallas. I'd never been involved in the business development process, and I was becoming a little intrigued by the idea. Besides that, I liked the idea of spending alone time with Elian, even though it was becoming increasingly more difficult to ignore the butterflies that showed up in my stomach every time I thought about that.

***

The plane ride was uneventful, and when I collected my luggage and started toward the exit, I saw a man outside the security panel holding a piece of paper with my name on it.

I walked over to him and with confusion asked, "You are looking for Martin Williams?"

"Yes, sir," he responded, "I'm your chauffeur."

"Chauffeur?" I questioned. "Who hired you? I wasn't aware a chauffeur would be waiting for me."

The man glanced at a piece of paper he'd brought with him and said, "Mr. Elian Whitman with Whitman Fine Dining is who hired me."

"That's who brought me here. I guess he just forgot to tell me about you."

The man shrugged, took my luggage from me, and led the way to the limo.

As I climbed into the back seat, I shook my head, thinking this was too much. I texted Elian when I got settled. "You didn't tell me about the limo part. I thought I was going to have a rental car."

Elian didn't reply right away. We were almost at the restaurant before I got a text back. "Sorry, I didn't want you to have to navigate traffic on a Friday night. I meant to tell you, but I've been in meetings all day. You have him all night, so if you want to go anywhere after the restaurant critique, feel free."

I texted Janice and told her I was almost there. She was standing in front of the building, and when she saw the limo, her eyes grew wide. "You are doing well!" she exclaimed as the chauffeur got out and opened the door for me.

"This wasn't my idea," I replied.

"I don't think it's a bad idea," Janice said, shaking her head.

"Good news: after dinner, my man here," I said as I patted him on the shoulder, "is on the tab to take us out wherever we wanna go."

Janice yelped and bounced up and down. "We're going dancing!"

"Apparently," I said with a smile. "Business first. Let's get unpacked, and then we'll get the work part out of the way."

We found the door to the upstairs rooms and—using the combination Elian gave me—went through the front door of his apartment.

We both stood in the doorway and gawked. The apartment was beautiful. It had been updated with exposed bricks and old plank hardwood floors. Elian had decorated the place with modern, yet comfortable décor. We walked in and found a note on the kitchen counter telling us the kitchen had been stocked, and the guest bedrooms were made up and ready for us.

We explored the apartment and found a room with a queen bed that was clearly the guest room, and then Elian's office that had a very nice blow-up mattress already made up for Janice.

"Looks like your man thinks of everything," Janice said with an impressed expression on her face. "If you don't want him, I think I do."

I popped her on the arm with the back of my hand.

"Back off, sister," I said. "I'm still pondering on the 'if I want him' part. Besides, he plays on my team, not yours."

"Clearly," she replied. "No straight man would own a place this tidy unless he could afford to hire staff.

She turned to me with squinted eyes. "He *is* so wealthy he has hired staff, isn't he?" she asked.

"I honestly don't know," I replied. "I ain't shopping for a man at the moment, and I don't really need a sugar daddy, so his financial standing hasn't been a relevant conversation."

"Sometimes I hate you, Martin," she said as she threw her arms around me for a bear hug.

"Okay, let's get ready so we can go play," she said before rushing off to her room.

I went into the guest room to change also, and smiled when I saw a mint had been placed on my pillow. Even though my first thought was the same as with the limo, *this guy is too much*, I couldn't help but be impressed at the same time.

The restaurant was similar in style to Elian's brewery that initially brought us together, both modern and warm at the same time. *So the man had a distinctive style. Good thing it was a nice style*, I thought.

The host was very young, I guessed around eighteen or so, but she was friendly and bubbly as she showed us to our table. She gave us both three menus and told us our server would be with us in a moment.

As promised, the server showed up within seconds after the hostess walked away. "Can I get your drink order?" she asked politely.

I said I'd stick to water until I knew what I was going to order, but Janice asked for a Long Island Iced Tea. When the server left, I said, "You're getting started early, I see."

"Of course I am," she replied. "We have a chauffeur and a limo to take us where we want. That means I can get sloshed and enjoy myself without having to worry about how I'll get home!"

I laughed at my friend. I knew work had been tough for her lately, so I was glad she was getting a chance to let her hair down.

I read through the menus. For the most part, I didn't like multiple menus. I thought they were confusing to customers. However, these seemed well designed. The first, larger menu was for food. The second was appetizers, and the third—which was the smallest but easiest to read—was desserts. The menus nested into each other, which meant they could be viewed separately or together. It seemed Elian had indeed taken my suggestion to focus on appetizers and desserts, not just the Tex-Mex food.

I excused myself from Janice and made my customary trek around the restaurant, pretending I was looking for the restroom but really checking the entire place out. I didn't see any customers who appeared upset, and most of the clientele were smiling and seemed to be having fun. I tried to see what most of the customers were eating, but it was a myriad of different types of food. I'd have to ask Elian for a breakdown on what foods were ordered the most.

When I went into the restroom, I checked the level of cleanliness and was impressed that, despite the fact that Elian wasn't around, the restroom was spotless. That was quite a feat at six-thirty on a Friday evening.

When I returned to the table, it was just in time for the server to show back up. "Have you decided what you want to order?" she asked pleasantly.

Janice allowed me to start the order, knowing from coming on these escapades with me in the past that I liked to direct the evening, so I could glean the most information out of the service as I could.

"No," I replied, "I just sat back down, but I have some questions." The server nodded. "What is the most popular menu item?" I asked.

"That depends," she responded. "Are you wanting appetizers or regular food?"

"Both," I replied.

"The most popular pairing is our Mexican spring rolls and taco salad."

"If you were going to order off the menu, what would you get?" I asked.

"I love the poppers myself," she said, "but I warn you, they are spicy."

"What do you think would go well with the poppers?" I asked.

"Ah, my very favorite menu item is the Yolanda chicken enchilada. I don't think you could go wrong there," she said.

"Great," I replied. "Give me just a few more minutes."

The server smiled and left. I purposefully took my time talking to Janice but pretended to be reading the menu as well.

One of the things I noticed first was the food she recommended wasn't the most expensive items but also wasn't the cheapest. I was impressed that she was honest with me and this wasn't a trained response to questions from customers.

Finally, after asking Janice if she was ready, I put my menu down and checked the time to see how fast the server responded to my cue that I was ready. We didn't have to wait long; the server showed back up within a few minutes. Janice ordered first, then I ordered, putting together a variety of items, substituting and adding in ways that were different from the way they were listed on the menu.

The server listened, repeated my order twice to ensure she had gotten my substitutions correctly, then headed to the kitchen.

In my experience, custom orders seldom came out correctly, so I was curious if Elian had trained his kitchen staff well enough to handle them.

The food came out in an appropriate amount of time. It was cooked well, and the customized order came out exactly as I'd ordered it. Naturally, I needed to complain to see how the reaction would be.

I immediately said, "I'm sorry, ma'am, but I ordered black beans, not pintos."

The server didn't hesitate. She responded, "Oh, no! I'll go fix that right now," and left, promising to return soon. Within a few minutes, she returned with a small bowl of black beans.

I smiled and said to Janice, "They almost always check their notes. Elian must have trained them not to do that. Questioning a customer over a small item like black beans is never a good idea."

Janice shook her head, "You are a dictator, Martin. I would hate to wait on you."

"Yeah, but since you are a corporate attorney, it is unlikely you ever will." Then, I stuck my tongue out at her, making her giggle.

Janice hadn't liked her Long Island Iced Tea because it was watered down, and the drink I ordered was a bit off as well, but I couldn't quite tell why. We sent both drinks back, and they came back with similar problems. We decided not to drink them, to see if the server would comp us since they weren't good.

We also both ordered dessert and again tried to stump the service and food prep with odd requests, but the desserts came out perfectly.

The server came back with the ticket, and the drinks hadn't been comped. I brought this to the server's attention, and she told us she'd see what she could do. When she came back, she apologized for the drinks and gave us a new bill with the drinks removed.

I asked to speak with the manager, and the server was clearly shocked but cordial, answering, "Of course. Let me go get her for you."

When she returned with the manager, I smiled and said, "I wanted to compliment you on the excellent service from this young lady. I also wanted to say everything tonight was perfect except the drinks, which our server comped for us."

The manager smiled, thanked me for the compliment, and apologized for the bad drinks. She said, "I can give you a coupon to come back for drinks again in the future. Maybe you'll have a better experience then."

Perfect response, I thought. *Not only does it compensate the customer for the bad service, but it pulls us back in to try them again after the problem is corrected.*

We paid our bill and left, going back up to Elian's apartment. "So, what were your thoughts?" I asked Janice.

"Overall, I'd say it is great. If I hadn't been with you, I'd have been happy. I wouldn't have even complained about the bad drink."

"If you came back, would you order another drink from them?" I asked.

She thought for a moment. "No, to be honest, I think I would have avoided buying a drink from them again. It was really watered down."

"That's the problem," I said. "When the rest of the service is almost perfect, and the drinks are bad, most people will ignore that, but then no one will reorder drinks in the future. That is a *huge* part of a restaurant's profitability. It's also a very important part of the dining experience."

"What were your thoughts?" Janice asked as she lounged back on Elian's black leather sofa.

"I thought it was perfect, except for the bar, of course," I replied. "I'd give it a four-point-five rating overall score."

"Me too," Janice said. Then, she jumped up and grabbed me and said, "I'm gonna go pee, then let's go dance!"

We partied the night away and didn't get back to the apartment until the wee hours of the morning. Janice was as plastered as she promised to be, and I wasn't far behind her. We both crashed on the queen bed in the guest room. When we woke the next morning, Janice's face was right in mine.

"Damn," I said, shaking Janice's shoulder to wake her. "Girl, you have rotten alcohol breath! Go brush your damned teeth!"

Janice turned over and said, "Fuck you, bitch." Then, she slowly got out of bed and went toward the bathroom.

When she came out, she plopped back on the bed, and said, "I'm happy you made me drink all that water last night, but I have *never* peed so much in my life. At least I don't have a hangover."

"You have ass breath, though," I said, teasing her.

"Fuck you," she said again as she reached over and grabbed my mint, which was sitting on the night table. She then popped it in her mouth.

"Hey, that was mine," I said, pouting.

"Finders keepers," she responded. "Let's go find something to eat. I'm famished."

The restaurant was closed until lunchtime, but we found a little bistro around the corner, ate, and gossiped for several hours. Luckily, the bistro wasn't very busy, and the server didn't seem to mind refilling our coffee. Before we finally got up to leave, we left the woman a nice tip for not kicking us out.

We slowly walked back to the apartment to get Janice packed and off to Austin for her date. When we arrived, Elian was there to meet us.

He greeted Janice with a cordial smile and asked if she'd had a good night before turning to me.

Janice was clearly enamored by Elian's natural sexual charm and stuttered a bit as she told him yes. "We went dancing after we ate at your restaurant," she said after she gathered her wits about her.

"I was hoping you'd take advantage of the driver," he told her.

Janice had found her footing, and as she walked toward the room where she'd left her stuff, she said, "Sorry, he wasn't really my type."

After she was out of earshot, Elian asked with a smile, "She is a character, huh?"

"Oh, man, you have no idea," I replied.

"Next time, I want to go out with you two."

After emerging again from her room, Janice hugged us both and gave me a kiss before leaving. "I love you more than sex," she said, and then jumped into her car, and drove away.

Elian reached over and took my hand. "You miss her, don't you?"

I hadn't really noticed the intimate gesture, being so caught up in the moment of my friend leaving and almost pulled my hand out of his before forcing myself to let it rest there.

"Yeah, we're really close. She pulled me through some rough times. I miss her a lot."

Elian let go of my hand and put his arm around me for a sideways hug. "I know how it feels to miss someone who makes you feel good inside. My best girlfriend is in Seattle. We've been friends since I was a little boy. We met before my family moved back to Fort Lauderdale."

Elian changed the subject and let his arm fall from my shoulder.

"Are you hungry? Do you want to grab something to eat?"

I chuckled. "No, we just walked back from the bistro around the corner."

"Oh," Elian said. "What did you think of it?"

"Not much really, just the run of the mill breakfast bistro. Not very busy for a Saturday morning, though."

"Yep, I agree. The owner has offered to sell it to me. I'm thinking about it."

"It wouldn't take much to improve it," I said.

Then, Elian became all business. "Shall we go back up to the apartment and discuss your experience last night at the restaurant? I'm anxious to hear what you thought."

"Sure." I shrugged as we walked up the steps.

Elian

So, spill. What were your thoughts?" I asked as soon as we sat down at the dining table.

"The restaurant is really nice. The ambiance is not unlike your brewery. The service was excellent, and I tried several ways to trip them up, but they held their own throughout the evening. I met the manager, and she was cordial and met my expectations. I see you took my suggestions about the appetizers and desserts, and those are top-notch. Your server even did a great job making parings when I asked her what she suggested. I could tell you've been training them how to make those without being obnoxiously over the top."

I smiled and said, "I'm glad that worked out. I was very anxious to hear how well that went for you. I was a bit afraid we would come off as pushy, putting the appetizers into the suggestions."

"No, not at all," Martin replied. "In fact, it made the experience more authentic, I think... especially since you didn't have your wait staff pushing the most expensive foods down people's throats."

I smiled again. "Yes, we let the server suggest the items they truly prefer the most. I thought, since we're asking them to pair either an appetizer or a dessert to the meals, they needed to be honest about their favorite parts of the menu."

"That was apparent," Martin said. "The desserts were also spectacular. I had the banana cream pie, and Janice had the fried cheesecake with strawberries. Both were perfectly prepared. I've had fried cheesecake before, and they used oil from their chips, and it wasn't very good. You must use a separate fryer for that."

Again, I smiled. "You are very good at this. Yes, we have a separate smaller fryer for our fried desserts. It cost a bit more, but since we are focusing on our appetizers and desserts, I thought I needed to make those perfect."

"Congratulations. You pulled it off," Martin remarked and smiled. His face suddenly became serious. "Not everything is perfect, though. The drinks were awful. Your wait staff and manager both apologized, and I was comped for the drinks when I complained. But if you don't remedy that, you are going to lose a lot of business."

"Can you tell me what was bad?" I asked.

"I can with Janice's—hers was very watered down. Mine was just off, but I'm not exactly sure what was wrong with it. Here is the problem you will face with your bar. Janice told me she wouldn't have complained about the drinks had I not been there because the rest of the service and food was so nice. I'm guessing that's the case with most of your customers, so if you have not received any complaints, that's probably why. However, I'm guessing your bar profits are dwindling. Am I correct on that?"

I was impressed. "Yes, we weren't sure why, but we've been steadily losing business in the bar. Last week was my worst, with profits well under half of what we were making."

"I'm not surprised people are returning to eat, yet avoiding your drinks. That has to be cutting into your bottom line," Martin said.

"You have no idea," I replied. "Are you willing to do something for me again? I have an idea to get to the bottom of this."

Martin agreed, and we both went down separately to the restaurant and ordered the same drink. After the drinks were served, we came back together and sat next to each other to taste the other's drink. We'd both ordered a chocolate martini, the most popular item ordered on Saturday afternoons. When we sat across from each other with our drinks, I requested that we exchange them.

Using a spoon, so as not to cross contaminate the drinks, Martin tasted mine first, and it was perfect. "Yum," he said as he put the spoon down.

"My turn," I replied.

I tasted it and immediately grimmaced. "Oh, that is awful! I don't even know what flavor is in there."

I stood up, waved the manager over, and asked her to taste each drink. She had the very same reaction I had when I tasted the second drink, the one Martin had ordered.

"I think it is time to have a discussion with our bartender. Wouldn't you agree?" I asked the manager.

"Martin, this could get ugly. Why don't you meet me back up at the apartment? I'll be back up to meet you in a moment."

Martin agreed and left.

When I went back to the apartment, Martin was asleep on the sofa.

I decided to allow him to sleep and wandered into the kitchen to prepare us both a little dinner. I'd arranged for all the grocery shopping to be done before Martin got here, hoping I'd be able to impress him with my cooking skills.

Of course, I'd planned to be cooking for three, but I was lucky enough to have Martin to myself tonight. My abuela had always said, "The way to a man's heart is through his stomach," so I prepared to do my best to test her theory out tonight.

Martin

I woke to the smell of onions and garlic frying. That was the most luscious smell in the world. I leaned up, stretching to see who was putting such an amazing aroma into the world. When I saw Elian cooking, both my heart and my groin lurched a bit. There were fewer things sexier to me than a hot man cooking in his kitchen.

Elian apparently knew what he was doing. It was clear that his sister had a knack for cooking, but I'd assumed Elian didn't. I self-reflected, realizing maybe I didn't think a man could be both business-minded and have the artistic techniques to create a good meal. Despite my prejudice against the businessman, the smells of onion and garlic certainly were a step in the right direction, and even if the food wasn't very good, the beautiful man was definitely good enough to eat.

Crap! I swore in my head, catching myself thinking of Elian as beautiful. Okay, truth be told, he was sexy as hell, but I quickly stamped my thoughts down. *No need going there. I'm spending the night alone with this man tonight, and we have an agreement to keep things business and platonic. Remember, platonic,* I reminded myself.

I stood up and walked into the kitchen. Elian looked over and flashed me that gorgeous smile of his. "I hope you're getting hungry. I decided to cook for you myself tonight instead of parading you through the city. Hopefully, you'll go easy on me since I'm not a pro like my sister is." He turned to put the marinated beef into the pan with the garlic and onions.

"I never complain when a man cooks for me. It is one of my favorite sights in the world. I'd rather see that than a stripper," I said with a self-conscious laugh.

Elian cocked an eyebrow at me, then hummed a stripping song, pretending to strip and flip the meat all at the same time.

"You are a goof," I said, teasing him. But the silly act had done more than a little to turn me on. Had things been different, I was almost sure poor Elian would have burned his meal after I did some of the things I was imagining to his body... things that involved him continuing with that sexy little dance.

I shook my head and turned to go back to the living room, giving myself time to clear the thoughts of bedding Elian out of my mind. As I turned, I asked, "So, what was the outcome of your meeting?"

Elian shook his head. "The bartender was inherited from the previous owner. In fact, I think they were having an affair. When the previous owner sold to me, she broke it off with him. Apparently, he's been using his position at the bar to get even with me. At least that is how he put it before he threw the bar towel at me and stomped out yelling he quit."

"He was deliberately sabotaging you?" I asked.

"It appears so," Elian replied. "Too bad, too, because he came highly recommended, and when he served *me* a drink, they were always top-notch."

"What are you going to do?" I asked.

"The manager has called in a favor from a man she used to work with. He is going to cover until we can find a bartender who doesn't want to chase off all our customers."

"I'm sorry that happened," I sighed.

"I'm just glad I had you come out this weekend. If we can fix this fast enough, I think we will save our bar business. I am going to be comping a lot of drinks for the next few weeks to build back our reputation," Elian sighed.

I nodded. "I think giving away a few good drinks to your repeat customers is a very good idea. Don't be surprised, though, if you have several people decline. You may need to make sure your wait staff is telling everyone you have a new barkeep. In fact, that could be the excuse for offering a free drink."

"Clever," Elian replied thoughtfully.

I yawned big and raised my arms over my head, causing my stomach to show under my shirt. When I glanced back at Elian, his face had gone from platonic to something very, *very* different.

"Um, where do you work out at?" he stammered.

I looked at him and, with a cocked eyebrow, asked, "Where did that come from?"

Elian blushed. "I noticed your abs when you were yawning," he replied. His face continued to turn a darker red from the awkward question.

I was enjoying the effect my stomach was having on Elian. The man seemed unflappable, but a little skin seemed to completely undo him. Yet, watching the man's reaction caused something to snap inside me as well. I'd been resisting my urge to kiss this guy since he'd showed up this morning, and his flustered awkwardness was the last straw.

I walked over to where he was cooking. Elian watched me with ever-widening eyes. I lifted my shirt over my abs, and then took it completely off. "I've been working out. All that restaurant food was going to turn me into a slob. What do you think?"

Elian gulped, and I chuckled low in my throat. "So, when is dinner going to be done?" I whispered in his ear.

"Um," was all Elian was able to get out, then he swallowed hard enough for me to hear.

"What?" I decided to play coy. "I just wanted to show you how I like to work out."

Again, Elian stammered but flipped off the heat under the pan. I laughed again, enjoying seeing this guy turned to mush over my body. I reached over and put my shirt back on, then leaned into Elian and kissed him square on the mouth.

"It is good to see you are as turned on by me as I am by you," I said, "but that doesn't mean we're going to do anything, Elian Whitman."

As I turned to leave, Elian spun me back around and kissed me deep and hard. This time, there was no civil peck; the kiss Elian gave possessed all the angst between us these past weeks. If I was going to pull back, it was going to have to be soon because Elian had just lifted the kiss to another level: tongue, saliva, and pure sexuality rolled into me like a storm surge in a category five hurricane.

Within an instant, my shirt was back off, and Elian's came off shortly after. We crossed the room, our kisses growing more passionate and desperate. Elian pushed me onto the sofa, and began assaulting my neck, then chest, and paused when he got to my nipples to nip ever so slightly. This was going to be raw sexuality, and Elian wasn't holding anything back.

Deep in the recesses of my mind, I could hear a faint cry from the part of my brain that told me to watch out—not to get close to a man again. *Especially this man, keep him at bay.* But instead of listening to that voice—which was just a little too easy to ignore—I responded to the need that Elian poured onto me.

Elian

All my hopes and wishes were being fulfilled, though I knew it might be too soon. I should have pulled back, but I wanted Martin so much. I wanted my mouth on him. I *needed* to taste him, feel him, be a part of him.

I unbuckled Martin's belt while my tongue assaulted his abdomen just above his pants. When I unbuttoned his pants and saw that he had gone commando, the lust inside me took over at such a thrilling discovery. I looked hungrily at Martin, and he responded to me with a sigh. I put my mouth on his cock, causing him to moan and buck up against me as I let my tongue explore his head.

Martin moaned with pleasure again when I found his slit, playing with it for only a moment while locking eyes with the beautiful man that lay before me. Then, I deep-throated him, not once but three times before pulling back and playing with his head again.

"Elian, OH MY GOD, it has been so long! I'm going to come. Oh God, I'm sorry, I'm coming!"

I pushed my mouth down over his cock and allowed his cum to burst into my mouth. Martin came so much that I choked a bit before I could swallow it all.

I'd always had a cum fetish, but I knew not every guy did. I slowly kissed my way back up to Martin's mouth, half-expecting him to turn away, but instead, he pulled me in for a deep kiss.

Martin

I could taste my own seed on Elian's tongue, which surprisingly, caused my dick to twitch back to life again.

I kicked my pants off, traded spaces with Elian on the sofa, and pulled his pants—that had somehow still remained on his body—off with one swipe. I slid Elian's cock into my mouth, and now that the intensity had eased a bit for me, I took my time exploring his beautiful and perfect-sized cock.

I knew before this night was over, I was going to have to convince Elian to put that in me. The thought caused me to get harder, and with renewed passion, I sucked on Elian's head before I moved down to his balls, pulling each into my mouth while my tongue explored the recesses below his sack.

When my tongue lightly touched Elian's hole, he moaned with pleasure, enticing me to use my finger to play with him while continuing to suck on his cock. I shivered as electricity shot through me from the intimate contact.

I wasn't a size queen by any means, but the size and smoothness of Elian's cock made exploring it that much more exciting. His balls and shaft were obviously sensitive, so while I fingered his ass, I moved my thumb into the base of his balls and massaged the area. I could tell the sensations were overtaking him, so I moved my mouth up and down his long, thick shaft, lightly playing with his head when I came back up to it.

"Do you have lube," I asked, "and a condom?"

Elian gave me a blank stare. I chuckled when it took him a moment to register what I was asking. "Not here," he said apologetically. "I wasn't prepared, sorry."

"No need, I can take care of this, but before the night is over, we are going to need to go to the drug store."

Elian nodded, then threw his head back when I deep-throated him again. Using my middle finger, I explored the soft insides of his hole until I found his prostate. Elian writhed with pleasure as I increased my movements, sucking his cock and stimulating his prostate until he pulled out of my mouth and came all over my face.

I smiled up at him, and he leaned over and kissed me. To my surprise, he licked his seed off my face, returning to my mouth between licks.

"God, that is so nasty it's hot," I said when he'd swallowed the last of it. We crawled naked into each other's arms and lay on the leather sofa, enjoying the afterglow of our sex. After a moment, I admitted, "You know, I'm hard as a rock. I could come again, but I'd rather wait until we have the right supplies."

Elian seemed to stop breathing for a moment. "If I had any idea this would have happened, I would have been prepared. I mean, I was going to try, but I figured you would push me away."

I laughed. "Good, I prefer to keep you off balance."

Elian lifted up on his elbow and said, "I'm going to have to watch my back." Standing up, he asked, "Are you ready to eat? I think dinner is... or was ready."

I'd forgotten about the food, but the moment Elian mentioned it, my stomach growled. "I guess I am," I said, and we both laughed.

We ate the meal in the nude, sitting on the floor in front of what I now thought of as the sex sofa. "I don't usually come so fast," I said with some embarrassment. "I haven't had sex since... well, for a long time."

Elian leaned over and kissed my cheek. "You rocked my world, Martin Williams. I've wanted to touch you for so long but had no idea how to convince you to let me." In an unforgettable moment, the beautiful man leaned his head onto my shoulder in a way that melted my heart.

"Clearly, you rocked mine, too," I laughed. "I should warn you, though... later, I'm going to do things to your body that will make you squirm. Then, I'm going to take that gorgeous cock of yours and ram it so far up my ass you will feel my vocal cords."

Elian froze, staring at me.

"Hey, you better eat up," I said, enjoying the expression on his face. "You are going to need your strength."

Enjoying the effect my words were having, I looked Elian in the eye and added, "I plan to use you over and over." I paused and placed a gentle kiss on his mouth before adding one more, "and over again."

It took Elian a moment to catch his breath. He put his fork and plate down, his expression serious. "Are you sure about all this? What made you change your mind?" he asked.

"You," I said, matter-of-fact. "You haven't pushed me. You tested the boundaries, of course, but never crossed them. That made me realize you were safe. I'm not saying I'm ready to get married, but I am ready to see what's here."

Elian looked at me with astonishment. "We both know I want you, he replied. "I really want you, but I can't say I'm not concerned about this sudden change of heart being too fast. Of course," he smiled ruefully at me, "if I'm being honest, I was going to seduce you this weekend, but I'm still reeling from this. I knew I screwed up with our first two dates."

I smiled. "I think for most guys that would've been less of a freak-out for them than it was for me. I've had a bad experience with my ex-boyfriend's family..."

"Yeah, mi tía told me she talked to you that night. I'm glad you're giving me a second chance, and I promise, Martin, I'm not going screw it up this time."

We put our plates in the sink and cuddled on the sofa for a while before I finally had to ask, "So, how far away is this drug store?"

Elian gave me a mischievous smile. "It is just around the corner."

"I'll tell you what," I said, "I'll stay here and clean up the dinner dishes, and you go to the store and get what we need."

"Deal," Elian said as he jumped up, threw his clothes on, and was out the door before I could get up.

"Glad to see he's eager," I said with a laugh.

Elian

By the time I'd returned, Martin was just finishing the dishes. I walked into the apartment and found him still butt naked but wearing my chef's apron. I laughed and said, "That has officially become my favorite apron."

Martin untied it, threw it over the kitchen chair, and came over to me. "You have too many clothes on," he said. "Let me help you take them off."

I was happy to oblige as Martin, once again, kissed my neck, lifted my shirt, bent down, and kissed my shoulders while playing with my nipples.

I took my shirt the rest of the way off and tossed it to the floor as Martin moved us toward the master bathroom. I continued stripping as we went. When we made it to the bathroom, I removed my pants, and turning the shower on, I pulled both of us in. I'd added a large two-person shower with a rainfall shower head when I had the room redone, so water streamed luxuriously over us as we soaped each other's bodies, paying special attention to our private parts.

I took the hand shower and rinsed Martin well, kneeling to take his cock into my mouth. Martin moaned as I ran my tongue over his head and slit. Water from above still washed down Martin's beautiful chest and into his pubic hair, enhancing the feeling of euphoria that had been building all evening. As I brought Martin to the point of ejaculation, I pulled back and stood up, spun him around, and—using conditioner—let my cock slide into the crease of his ass. Martin shuddered at the feeling of my cock tempting his hole. I was happy giving or receiving, but I knew there was no way this evening would end without my cock being inside of him.

I rinsed Martin's ass, then kneeling once again I began to assault his sensitive area with my tongue. Slowly at first, then moving along the ridges between his balls and his ass, licking up toward his hole. Slowly, excruciatingly slowly, I allowed my tongue to slip into the edges of that tight rim.

Martin cried out with pleasure. "No one, not even my ex, has ever done that to me, Elian. Fuck, I could come again."

I had a mission, and when he reached for his cock, I knocked his hand away. "Not yet, mi amor. Let me make love to you."

Martin

I was sure I was going to melt into the shower and down the drain as Elian picked up the intensity by thrusting his tongue into my hole, causing my muscles to contract, then loosen.

"I think you are ready for me," Elian said as he stood up. "Can I make love to you, Martin?"

I was so lost in ecstasy all I could do was nod. Elian pulled me out of the shower, toweled me off, and led me to the bed.

I lay on my side, watching Elian as he put the condom on and lubed up. Elian kissed me before rolling me over, and finally spooning me. He slowly rubbed my hole with his cockhead, teasing my opening until I was writhing with pleasure.

Elian whispered in my ear, "I want my cock in you. I want you so bad, baby. I want to hear you beg for it." His words sent a shudder down my back and echoed in my cock, which hardened even more.

"Please," I begged, "please fuck me, Elian."

Elian's cock caught in my opening. He gently pressed, causing me to moan again, "Fuck me Elian, fuck me, please."

As his head breached me, I sucked in a deep breath and tensed.

"Let me in, Martin. Push out on me. Let me fill you, baby."

I moaned again and pushed my ass up against him, allowing the head to fully slip into me.

"Shh, not too fast!" Elian mummered. "Mi guapo, slowly push out against my cock."

I did as Elian instructed. He pulled out slowly, allowing the taught muscle to expand and contract around his head, not pulling all the way out but enough that I was experiencing pleasure and not pain.

Elian slipped his tongue into my ear, which caused me to writhe again. "I can't wait, Elian. I want you in me so bad."

"I will, I will, baby. Just take your time." Elian slid his cock back and forth until I relaxed around him, and I began moving in rhythm with him.

After Elian had loosened me up, he told me to turn over onto my back. While lifting my legs, he guided his cock back into me, again taking time to allow me to get used to this position.

I called Elian's name as he entered me. I wanted nothing more than for him to thrust into me hard, fucking me, taking ownership of me, but Elian was clearly restraining himself, taking his time.

He slowly worked his cock in and out, but I'd finally lost all patience, and demanded, "FUCK ME NOW!"

Elian complied, and thrust his cock fully into my ass as I roared with pleasure. "Fuck me, Elian, FUCK ME!" I demanded as he continued pounding my ass. The pleasure was so overwhelming, I felt my eyes roll into the back of my head.

Elian pulled out of my ass and urged me to get on all fours. I complied as quickly as I could.

Slipping his cock into my ass again, Elian began to pound me doggie-style. He leaned over me, his warmth wrapping around me as he whispered in my ear, "Querido, you are so tight, you feel so good." Impossibly, his words and the weight of his body pressing on mine made me want him even more.

Elian

"Oh my God, I'm going to come!" Martin writhed beneath me, meeting my thrusts.

"Me too, baby," I groaned, riding the initial feelings of ecstasy.

The next time I hit Martin's prostate, he burst all over the bed. As he came, his ass tightened around my cock, sending me over the edge as well. We both continued to spasm as I gently pulled out, grabbing the condom to prevent it from leaking. I kissed his back. "One moment, baby, I'll be right back." I tossed the condom into the trash can by the bathroom door, then quickly wet a washcloth and returned to wipe us both down.

"Oh my God," Martin said when I returned. "It's been so long. I forgot how incredible that feels."

I stared down at the beautiful man. "It can get even better than that," I said.

I fell next to him and we lay in each other's arms as our hearts slowly stopped racing and the euphoric afterglow kicked in.

Martin nuzzled into my chest, dozing first, which only caused my heart to swell more. It'd been a while since I'd felt this way about any man. In fact, I couldn't remember ever wanting a man as much as I did this one. To have him come to my bed, despite having trust issues around men, both shocked and pleased me.

I still had a nagging feeling in the back of my mind that we had moved too fast. I feared that Martin would wake up and try to run. If he did, though, I knew I'd not be far behind him. No, I wasn't going to give up on Martin Williams; the man not only intrigued me, but I was beginning to crave the time we spent together.

If fact, I thought about him constantly when we were apart. Was I obsessed? Maybe a little, but experience had taught me to trust my instincts when I became this attached to someone or something as they rarely led me wrong. I resolved if needed, I'd bide my time until Martin was ready to take this to the next level.

Martin

When I awoke, I was pleasantly surprised to find myself cuddled into Elian. Clichéd as it might be, we seemed to fit together perfectly.

"Did I snore?" I asked, sensing that he was awake.

"No, but I could tell you were asleep," Elian chuckled.

"Afterglow sleep is the best sleep in the world," I sighed.

"It is," Elian agreed. "The only thing better is watching your lover sleep in love's afterglow."

I squirmed a bit in discomfort at the word love, even though I realized he did not mean it in the big four-letter-word sense. I talked myself down, though, and let the comment slide. No need to ruin a perfect evening with fear of the big L-word.

"You are good at it, you know?" I said.

"What's that?" Elian asked.

"Lovemaking. I think I'm pretty bad at it. I've been around, but my experiences are limited to hooking up and an ex-fiance."

Elian laughed. "As I recalled, you seemed to do a pretty good job with it just a moment ago."

I smiled and snuggled into him again.

We spent the rest of our time in Dallas making love with the occasional stop for food. Luckily, we had the same flight back to Fort Lauderdale, and our seats were together in business class. We held hands almost the entire way back, cuddling together like obsessed teenagers.

As we were getting ready to land, I switched my phone on and looked at my schedule to make mental plans for when I could see Elian again.

"Are you free this week for a review of a new Cuban restaurant a couple miles from my office?"

Elian shifted uncomfortably and said, "I can't go with you on that review."

I frowned at him puzzled and pressed him for more information. "I'm sorry, Martin," he replied. "You are going to have to trust me on this one."

I shrugged and decided to drop it, trusting he'd fill me in later.

We exited the plane, gathered our luggage, and then found Elian's car in the garage. When we climbed in, I glanced at Elian for a moment and said, "Just remember, if you invest in any of the restaurants under my watch, you have to let me know ahead of time. I can't afford to be seen as playing favorites, Elian."

"I know," Elian replied. "It isn't that, but you have to trust me that I am a little too close to this one to join you."

"No problem," I replied, smiling. "I just wanted you to remember our agreement."

Elian leaned over and kissed me. "I finally got you where I want you, hermoso. I'm not going to throw it away by reneging on our deal. Well, not that part of the deal. The being real boyfriends part, that one's off the table."

I grinned at Elian before kissing him back. "I think you are handsome, too. And I might've been a bit overly careful on the pretend boyfriend part."

The drive back to my apartment was sweet. It felt so good to enjoy Elian's company. I invited Elian to stay awhile, but he declined, saying he had work to catch up on before the morning workday.

I put on some charm, saying, "I promise you won't regret it."

Elian laughed. "Okay, but for just a minute, then I really have to go."

When we got into my apartment, I tugged Elian into my bedroom and began stripping him, kissing the parts of his skin as I exposed them.

Elian sucked in a breath as I kissed his abdomen just above the waist of his pants. I gazed up at him and beamed right before I rubbed my tongue under his waistband as I slowly unhooked his belt. I ran my hands up his naked torso, stopping to play with his nipples, which I had learned was an especially erogenous area for him. I returned my hands to unbutton his pants, and when they fell to his feet, I was surprised to find that Elian had gone commando.

"You naughty dog," I said, as Elian chuckled.

"Just trying to make it easier on you," he said.

I nosed into his groin and began a thorough exploration of the area. I licked around the base of his cock, then gently sucked his balls into my mouth one at a time. My tongue explored every sensual inch of him without touching his now-quivering shaft and leaking head.

I pushed Elian gently to the bed and crawled back up to kiss him on the mouth, retracing my steps back down his beautiful body. Finally, I lifted Elian's legs one at a time, removing his shoes, then his taking his pants the rest of the way off. I let my mouth move slowly up the inner parts of his thigh where I nibbled and teased, causing him to strangle a sob.

I caressed his balls with one hand, pulling them up slightly so my tongue easily reached beneath them to explore the sensitive area between his sac and his hole. I licked upward firmly, pressing my tongue against the base of his shaft with every upstroke. Elian writhed with pleasure. "I want you to fuck me," he moaned.

I stopped short. After our first bout of playing with each other, Elian hadn't shown much interest in switching positions. I'd assumed maybe he wasn't into being a bottom, but the thought of fucking him sent shivers up my spine and blood coursing into my cock.

F"Maybe if you are a good boy," I teased.

"Mi amor, you're evil," Elian sighed.

I chuckled as I slipped Elian's cock into my mouth. He drew in a breath while I sucked his head, taking my time playing with his slit, teasing the opening with the tip of my tongue.

"Oh God, that feels good," he whimpered. Just when I could tell Elian was settling into the sensation, I took his whole cock into my mouth. His abdomen stiffened, and his moans grew louder.

I slowly moved my tongue up and down his cock. Using the saliva that had dripped from my mouth to moisten my finger, I rubbed around Elian's balls, teasing him with a light touch.

I slowed my mouth's exploration of his cock as I slid my finger beneath his sac to play with the sensitive area around his hole. I didn't try to penetrate him yet; instead, I worked to give him the most pleasure I could from the sensation of being touched so intimately.

Elian's hands were in my hair. He begged in a whisper I barely heard, "Please Martin, *por favor.*"

Unable to resist his plea, I began sucking harder as I slipped my finger into the tight hole.

"Oh God, Martin, I want you so bad," Elian cried. As he squirmed, I pressed my finger farther into him, feeling the taut ring of muscle fight against the intrusion.

Using his resistance to increase the sensation, I shifted positions so that I was lying between his legs, jacking him off with my hand. I slipped under Elian, pressed his legs up to his shoulders, and thrust my tongue into his tight hole.

Although I could feel his muscle rebel, I could tell he was in ecstasy. "Oh my God, I have never wanted anyone so bad," he murmured.

As I worked the sensitive puckered skin, the muscle began to relax, allowing me to replace my tongue with a wet finger moving in and out of his hole, causing him to moan more and more with each new invasion.

Once I could slip a third finger in, I slowly crawled out from under him and pulled the nightstand drawer open to get the lube and a condom I'd stored there.

I used the lube on Elian's ass, starting again with one finger, then two and a third, allowing him to get used to the sensation of the lube.

"I want you to fuck me *right now*, Martin!" Elian exclaimed, causing me to chuckle.

I leaned over to kiss him. "I'm going to fuck your tight hole so hard, Elian," I said in his ear.

"Oh God, *get in me!*" he exclaimed, grabbing and holding me by the shoulders.

I couldn't help the goofy grin that came across my face as I pulled the condom on and pressed my cock to him. Slowly, using my hand to push the head against his hole. I was struggling to go slowly. I didn't want to hurt him but I also knew at this point, I was too far gone to tolerate slow.

My cockhead continued to put pressure on his ass, and Elian shifted so he could push himself harder onto me, forcing my cock to go in faster than I would've done.

"I said fuck me now!" he demanded and pressed down against me.

Sliding into Elian so quickly sent lust surging through me, driving me into sexual madness. When I pulled out this time I thrust full force into him, causing him to suck in his breath and then yell, "Thank God. Fuck me, Martin, FUCK ME!"

I slammed my cock into him, struggling to hold my release.

"You are so fucking hot, Elian! Damn, you are so fucking hot!" I moaned the words as I thrust into him again and again.

"God please, Martin, fuck me harder!" he exclaimed, and I complied, thrusting harder and harder into his ass, losing myself to this new sensation.

I pulled out and repositioned Elian on all fours and came back onto him doggie-style. Slowly slipping back into him, I rubbed my hands over his beautifully muscled back.

Then, I began to pound him.

"God, that feels so good, Martin. I love the feel of your cock in me." The sound of his pleasure caused me to hard

en even more, and I shoved myself into his tight ass even harder.

I shifted slightly, thrusting downward so that I'd come closer to hitting Elian's prostate. As I hit my mark, he arched up in surprise. "Oh God, that's it, that's it," he moaned.

I repeatedly hit his prostate until he cried. "I'm going to come, Martin. I'm going to come."

"Show me, baby. I want to watch you."

As I said this, Elian exploded all over my bed. His ass contracted with the ejaculation.

I shuttered, yelling, "Oh God, oh God, your ass is so tight, Elian!" as I emptied myself inside of him.

When I pulled out, I fell onto the bed.

We both panted, holding each other as we slowly allowed ourselves to calm down.

"I didn't think you were a bottom," I said.

"I'm versatile, but I haven't bottomed much," Elian said and smiled at me. "But all the way home from Dallas, all I could think of was your cock in my ass."

I beamed back at him. "Was it as good as you were hoping?"

"Oh no," Elian said, causing me to frown. He put his hand up to my face and traced the frown with his finger. "It was better than I could have imagined." Then, he leaned over and kissed me hard on the lips.

Elian

"When do I get to fall in love with you?" I asked, waiting to see if Martin freaked out.

The shock on his face was amusing. "Well, not yet. There are rules about these kinds of things."

I laughed and replied, "*Mi amor*, I need to know those rules before I say something you don't want to hear."

Martin leaned up on his elbow and rested his hand on my forearm. "I think we both have feelings, but we seriously have to take it slow. Okay?" The look Martin gave me revealed more vulnerability than I think he realized. I could tell if I pushed a bit further, I was taking a chance of chasing him away.

"I know," I replied. "I just needed you to know, this isn't just sex for me. I like you a lot, Martin, and there will be a lot more to this than me liking you if we keep going."

Martin sat up on the side of the bed, looking away from me. "You know I've been burned, Elian, and had that not happened, I'm sure I'd be all yours. I'm not one to put the brakes on emotions, so don't think I'm standing by convention, but you have to give me time." He turned back to me then and said, "So, is fucking you all it takes to get a ring on my finger?"

I felt my eyes grow wide at the change of mood, and I reached over and began tickling him. "I may be easy, Martin, but you don't have to throw it in my face."

He laughed and squirmed. "Hey, no fair. No tickling!"

"All's fair in love and war," I replied as I reached down and kissed his sexy lips.

"I'll remember that," Martin said over my kiss. "Do you really have to go now?"

"Yeah, I have another damned meeting tomorrow morning with my board. They are giving me all kinds of grief about the Dallas restaurant, but now, thanks to you, I can show them a very sweet upswing in our bottom line. The best part is I can tell them why our drink sales were declining. Tomorrow will be an exhausting but good day."

"So, no nookie tomorrow night then?" he asked.

"Nookie?" I laughed at the antiquated word. "I'm always game for nookie," I replied.

"I won't be working tomorrow night. When are you done?"

"It'll be late, maybe eightish?"

"Where's your meeting?" Martin asked.

"I'm meeting in the boardroom at my uncle's office, which is across the street from the condos."

"I can meet you down there if you like," Martin said.

"Deal. Meet me at eight-thirty at my uncle's bar. We can make plans from there."

Martin

We met as often as possible as the week wore on. I could tell we were getting closer, and with that closeness came a feeling of dread. I found myself waiting for the other shoe to drop.

I knew intellectually this had nothing to do with Elian and everything to do with Matilda the Hun, my ex's mom, but I couldn't help thinking it was just a matter of time before Elian flipped out and left me.

If that happened again, it would shatter what was left of my heart into pieces and I'd never be able fit them back together again. All that being said, my friends had helped me see that this man needed a chance of his own—not to be held accountable for other people's stupid actions.

Thursday night came, and I took Kristine with me to the Cuban restaurant Elian had said he couldn't review with me. We arrived at approximately six p.m., which we knew should be the peak time. There were several people waiting out front when we arrived, and several were already leaving.

I asked a couple who was leaving what was going on, and they said they had a reservation for five-thirty, but were not checked in until five forty-five, "and we've been waiting since then." The husband said irritably. I ooked around and although the restaurant appeared empty, they clearly weren't seating any of the customers.

Kristine and I proceeded to the front desk but waited over fifteen minutes for the hostess to arrive to take our names, much like the couple who left had told us. When I confronted the hostess about the wait time and the empty seats, she was rude to me, smacking her gum in my face and telling me if I couldn't wait I should go somewhere else. Then, she tossed her hair and left the front area again.

I walked around the partition, pretending I was searching for the restroom and found the hostess leaned over the bar, talking to one of the bartenders and twirling her hair, ignoring the front desk completely.

I went back and confided with Kristine what I'd seen. "Shall we just leave now, and you report that you didn't get to eat because of the horrible front desk staff?" she asked.

"No, it's possible this is just a personnel problem. It's a new place, and finding good help, especially for a host position, can be tough. Let's give them another chance," I replied.

One hour later, we were finally seated. It took another fifteen minutes for anyone to take our drink order, and when it finally came, it was wrong. Kristine had ordered a margarita, and I'd ordered white wine. They brought Kristine three shots of tequila and me a beer.

When I told the server her mistake, she argued with me, saying she wrote down exactly what we ordered. Kristine stood to leave, but I took ahold of her hand and asked her to sit.

"When it's this bad, it deserves a full review," I said, trying to convince her to stay. "Think of all the people we are going to save from a horrible experience."

Reluctantly, she sat back down, arguing, "Martin, I've gone on too many of these with you to count. I have never had this bad of an experience. I shudder to think what the food will be like."

"It's going to be horrible, of course, but we are going to sit here and give them the benefit of the doubt because that's what we do," I said with a chuckle. "Sit back and enjoy. You can help me trash them tomorrow in my critique."

We both decided to order something simple, something that every Cuban restaurant should do well. "Maybe they are having a bad night, or maybe the boss isn't here," I suggested to Kristine. "At least they should have a chance to prepare something delicious."

It took way too long for the server to return, and she was still in a huff about the drink mix-up, which incidentally, she refused to correct. We both ordered Cuban-style grilled chicken with a side of black beans and rice, and repeated the order to our server twice just to make sure she heard us correctly. It took another forty-five minutes for the food to arrive. Although the order was correct this time, it was cold and the chicken had dirt and a hair on it. Kristine snapped a photo of the food and stood up to find the server.

"This is seriously too much!" she exclaimed. At first, the server ignored her, which only made her more upset.

When the woman did finally come back, Kristine was irate. "There is a hair on the chicken and what appears to be dirt," she said.

"Well, it ain't my hair," the server said with an attitude.

Kristine's face was taking on a crimson shade of red. I was afraid she was about to burst a blood vessel, so I decided to chime in before something did happen.

"Young lady, please go get your manager for me."

The woman looked at us and said, "No."

"That's fine," I said calmly. "Then, would you please let him or her know that I will be contacting the health department tomorrow morning. I will also be forwarding them a picture of the food with the hair and dirt on it that clearly shows it was dropped on the floor, then picked back up to be served to my friend here. You also need to let him or her know that you refused to allow them to explain this horrible night and the actions of their staff. Did you get all that, or should I write it down for you?"

The woman turned in a huff and rushed into the kitchen. As we walked toward the front door, a man in his mid-thirties burst through the door and stepped in front of us.

"You haven't paid for your meal," he demanded.

"That's true," I replied. "Can you tell me if you would like us to pay for the drinks we didn't order and therefore didn't drink or the food that obviously fell on the floor?" I was beginning to feel my own ire kick up. "Which one do you want us to pay for, sir?"

Before the man could reply, the dining room erupted in applause. I turned around, surprised that I had an audience.

When I turned back, the man stood in my way and said, "If you try to leave, I will call the police."

"Then, by all means." I pulled my wallet out and gave him a credit card.

Anticipating the possibility of this, I'd given the man the card that had my paper's name on it. Usually, I like anonymity, but tonight, I wanted the man to see

I was a reporter. The man didn't notice the card until he ran it through and handed me the receipt.

"You... you are with the *Fort Lauderdale Press*?" he asked.

"Yes, we both are," Kristine replied with indignation. "I'm an editor at the paper, and this gentleman is a food critic for the downtown area." The man's face turned pale as he returned the card.

"If... if I had known you were coming..." he stammered.

"Then you'd have pretended to be a decent place to eat?" I interrupted. "Your staff has been abysmal all evening. We arrived at six p.m. It is now almost nine, and we still haven't eaten."

Kristine chimed in then. "I have been in this business a long time, sir, and this is hands down the worst experience I've ever had."

We both turned to leave as the man stepped back in front of us. "You can't give us a bad review," he replied, panic in his voice.

"Sir, you need to move away from us, or it will be me calling the police," Kristine said.

"I would move away from the door if I were you," I added.

The man hesitated before moving, but he finally did, and we left the restaurant.

"Let's get a move on before that bully comes after us with a weapon," Kristine said.

I agreed and added, "Meet me at the office. We can square up there before we head home, just in case these nutcases follow us."

When we got to the office, we both sat down and recounted the events of the evening to ensure we didn't miss anything. It was important we both remembered what happened and that the events were documented immediately following the visit to ensure accuracy.

This was going to be the worst review I'd ever written, and from the way the guy acted as we were trying to leave, I was sure there was going to be fallout from it. It was best to ensure we had all our ducks in a row before taking this on.

It was close to midnight when I got home. I knew I wouldn't be able to sleep, so I texted Elian to see if he was still awake.

Within moments, Elian responded. "Yep, just watching TV. How was the restaurant?"

I waited a moment, then dialed the phone. When Elian answered, I asked, "What is your involvement with the restaurant?"

"I don't have any. Why?" he asked.

"Because you never refuse to come eat with me," I said. "I know something's up."

Elian hesitated, finally saying, "I don't want to influence your review. It is what we agreed to. If I'm involved in any way, I'll step out. I am not financially involved, Martin, but I do know the owner."

"Then you need to give him a heads-up that I'm about to write the worst restaurant review I have ever written."

Elian was quiet but finally asked, "Was it that bad?"

"If you know him," I replied, "then I can't go into detail, but I wasn't the only one there. Kristine was with me... Elian, it was the worst dining experience I have ever had.."

Elian's voice got quiet, and he said, "I understand, Martin. Try to get some rest."

"I will," I replied, and then hung up.

I was sad. I really hated writing bad reviews. All the hopes and aspirations that go into a new restaurant could be dashed by a bad review. I'd often—when something was horrible—gone back to give the staff and the restaurant a second chance.

Most of the time, though, bad was bad, and there wasn't much to do other than tell the truth. I knew a review like this one could be the final straw that shut the business down. You can't serve people food that has been on the floor. It was against all restaurant ethics. It was the ultimate betrayal of a customer's trust. I had no choice but to report it as it had happened. That is exactly how I did all my reviews, truth and accuracy—the code of journalism.

I also had a sinking feeling this wasn't just someone Elian knew. I wouldn't believe Elian would lie to me. If he had ownership, he'd admit he had ownership, but my Spidey senses told me this wasn't just anyone, it was someone important.

I tossed and turned throughout the night. The next morning, I got up early, made a pot of coffee, and drank the whole thing. Then I went to the office and began drinking a second pot. I sat down, reviewed the notes Kristine and I wrote the night before, and wrote my review, highlighting each specific event. Most importantly, I drilled the issue of trust between kitchen staff and customers. "It's never okay to serve food that you know could harm a customer," I wrote. "That kind of behavior is the ultimate ethical breach for a restauranteur." That tenet was my main point of the review.

I sent the critique to Kristine to review, and I went into our blog and gave the restaurant my first-ever zero out of five stars. I pressed enter and sat back waiting for the fireworks to hit.

After it was done, I went to Kristine's office and asked, "What did you think of the review?"

She glanced over and nodded. "It was harsh, but it was honest. That's what counts."

"I need a drink," I said.

"You better watch your back for the next few days," she responded. "This is the kind of review that puts restaurants out of business."

"Speaking of that, did you contact the health department?" I asked.

She nodded again. "This isn't the restaurant's first infraction. They are doing a full investigation. I've already emailed the pictures to the investigator."

"I wasn't joking," she added. "You need to lay low for a while. How long has it been since you were home?"

I looked at her surprised. "You think I'm in real danger?"

"It's possible," she said. "I'd rather be safe than sorry. A week back home would do you good, and meanwhile, this could have some time to blow over."

"Maybe you're right. I'll see if I can get Elian to go with me. I'd like him to meet my parents anyway."

"This is the time to do it," Kristine replied. "Take two weeks. If it hasn't calmed down by then, I'll let you know."

Kristine stood up and hugged me. "I'm proud of you. This situation sucked, but you did a great job with the review. Very respectful and professional."

"Thanks, Kristine," I said. "It doesn't make it easier that I'm the voice that shuts this place down, but I couldn't ignore it either."

"Nope, you couldn't," she replied.

The next day was a shitstorm. The health department closed the restaurant down by noon, which caught the attention of the evening news. A TV news reporter from the news channel contacted Kristine for an interview, but she declined for both of us. She told them that if they wanted her to, she could contact some recent customers who'd commented on our blog to see if they would be willing to sit for an interview.

As it turned out, most of them were willing, and the news channel set up a panel as each person shared their experiences that evening.

The next morning, I got a text from Elian asking if I was okay.

"Yeah, but I'm going to head out of town for a while. Is there any way I can get you to come with me? Wanna meet the parents?"

Elian wrote back a few minutes later. "Oh God, that really is scary isn't it?"

"You bet it is," I responded, "but you owe me not one visit but *two!*"

"Damn, I do, don't I?" was Elian's reply.

"Oh yeah, baby, and I'm going to have my parents invite the entire Williams gang, too. Turnabout is fair play, beautiful!"

"When do I have to face the music?" Elian texted back.

"Soon, but I'll call home and see. Maybe this weekend or the following?"

"Sure, I'm all yours. I can drive up from Dallas. Wanna meet for coffee this morning? I have a midmorning meeting but want... *need* to see you! I miss you so bad!"

"Sure, meet you at my office in an hour?" I asked.

"Sure, see you there," Elian replied.

I danced around my apartment as I called my parents. Mom answered in a sleepy voice.

"Did I wake you up?" I asked.

"Yeah, but I was about to get up. Everything okay, honey?" she asked.

"Yeah, so you know, I'm coming home, but I wondered if I could bring my boyfriend, at least for a little while. I think you'll like him."

I could hear shuffling in the background, and when my mom spoke again, I could tell I was on speaker.

"We didn't know you had a boyfriend, dear," she replied.

"Is he rich?" my dad asked, also with a sleepy voice.

"John," I heard my mother chastise. I laughed.

"Sorry Dad, I don't really know his net worth, but he doesn't seem to be struggling any."

"Then sure, you can bring him," Dad chortled.

"What's his name, honey?" Mom asked.

"Elian, Elian Whitman," I replied.

"We look forward to meeting him," my parents said in unison.

"Okay, I gotta go, y'all. We are meeting this morning for coffee before work. I really think you are going to like him."

"If you like him, honey, then we'll like him," my mom said.

I skipped through my morning routine and decided to spring for a cab instead of taking the little scooters to work like I usually did. When I got to the coffee shop, I could see Elian in the window. He was talking to some muscle-bound, dark wrestler-looking guy whose voice was so loud I could hear him before going into the shop.

When I walked in, the man turned around and upon seeing me, sprang to his feet and lunged at me. If Elian hadn't been right behind him, I was sure I'd have been beaten to a pulp. Elian grabbed the muscle man and literally shoved him past me and out the front door.

"Go the fuck home, you idiot!" Elian yelled at the man.

"Not until I put that busybody's mouth in the back of his throat!" the man yelled back.

"If you lay a hand on him, it will be last time you see that hand!" Elian said with a force that rocked both the man and me.

"Just 'cause you are fucking him doesn't mean he can go making up lies about my restaurant and getting me shut down!"

"He didn't shut your damned restaurant down, you idiot. Your damned girlfriend did that, along with your inability to hire reliable staff."

The man eyed Elian with pure anger, but he refused to back down. He didn't challenge Elian again but peered into the coffee shop window where the rest of the patrons and I stood watching and said, "This isn't over, pipsqueak. He can't protect you all the time."

Elian flipped the man around and punched him in the face, knocking him to the ground. In a voice that was so low I could barely hear it, Elian said, "Don't you ever threaten him again. Do you hear me?"

The man got to his feet, then lunged at Elian, about to hit him, then something shifted in his gaze, and he backed off. Locking eyes with me again with an angry glare, he flipped me the bird.

Elian rushed back into the coffee shop and to my side. "Are you okay?" he asked.

"No," I replied, "not really. Who was that man?"

"He was the owner of the restaurant you reviewed."

"Why didn't he hit you, Elian?" I asked, glaring at him with suspicion.

"Because he is my cousin, and if he hit me, he'd have the entire family after him."

It took only a moment for the information to digest. "He is your *Alverez* cousin?" I asked, holding my arms up as a warning for him not to approach me.

Elian averted his gaze and responded, "Yeah, he is my Alverez cousin."

"Shit," I said and walked to the door.

"Wait," Elian said, but I beelined it to the office. "Wait, he's an idiot! We all know he is an idiot. Don't take it out on me!"

I turned back to Elian as I came to the edge of my office building.

"I'm not taking anything out on you. I just found out the worst review I've ever done was on a restaurant owned by the cousin of the man I've been sleeping with. And not only a cousin, but a cousin who is more like a brother. You two live in the same building, for God's sake. I bet you even spent the evening with his parents last night, didn't you?" I accused.

Elian slowly nodded again, but continued to stare at the ground.

"Did you know my ex left me because his fucking mother was out to get me? Did you know that I've mourned the loss of a man who turned against me for his family when I didn't do a damned thing wrong? No, you didn't know that because I haven't told you, and you know why I didn't tell you that? Huh? Do you know, Elian?" I forced myself upon Elian with my finger poking into his chest.

"I didn't tell you because you are so fucking close to your damned family. Why didn't you tell me that I was reviewing your fucking cousin's restaurant, you idiot? Why would you put me between you and them?" I asked incredulously.

Elian tried to pull me into his arms. "Oh, no, you don't get to touch me. You don't get to see me or come around me again, Elian. I'll not be put back in that spot, not by you, not by anyone." I could feel my face had gone from emotional to stone cold. "I don't ever want to see you again."

Elian's face was full of panic as he once again tried to move toward me. I put my hand up and said, "*Ever,*" then turned and walked away.

I went into my office, closed the door and blinds, and cried for a full hour before Kristine finally knocked. "I'm coming in, Martin," she warned, and then opened the door.

She pulled the chair from across the desk to sit next to me and pulled me into her arms. I thought my tears were spent, but as soon as my friend hugged me, the tears began to fall again. "I know," she said. "Just so you are aware, there is a video of you, the meathead, and Elian online. There are already over a thousand views. I'm guessing this is going to go viral."

"God, I hate him," I said through snot and tears.

"Oh, honey, there are over a thousand people who hate him. By tonight, it is probably going to be a million people who hate him."

"Not the meathead," I said to her. "Elian. I hate him for letting me fall in love, then putting me between his fucking cousin and my job."

"Oh," Kristine said but didn't say more.

"What?" I replied. "Why did you just say 'oh?'"

Kristine scooted back a bit but left her hand on my shoulder.

"Well, honey, didn't you have an agreement that if Elian was involved, he'd back off?"

"Yeah, but we didn't have an agreement that he'd feed me to the wolves."

"No," she chuckled. "But would you have been upset if he'd have told you? Wouldn't that have come off as him trying to influence you?"

I didn't want to answer. I wanted to be mad. I didn't want to think I was wrong about this. I'd ended things with Elian and that hurt me to my core.

"I'm going to go home to Austin today I think, Kristine. I've already booked the flight."

"Good," she said. "I'm going to go with you back to your apartment to keep an eye on you in case the meathead comes back. Then, I'll take you to the airport. I'll feel better when you are on a flight out of Fort Lauderdale."

I sighed, then laid my head down on my desk. "I can't catch a break with men, Kristine. I think my heart is broken more this time than it was after Peter."

"I'm sorry, sweetie. This never gets easier," she sighed.

Kristine was as good as her word. She drove me home, helped me pack, and finally drove me to the airport.

"Have a nice vacation, honey, and don't think about all this stuff. It'll work itself out," she said.

We hugged outside the terminal. "We love you, dear Martin. All of Fort Lauderdale loves you. Everyone is on your side with this one, and when you get yourself back together, we will want you back. Do you hear me?" she asked.

"Yes, of course," I replied. "I'm not going to let the meathead, *or* his cousin, chase me away. I love Fort Lauderdale, too."

"That is what I wanted to hear," Kristine said with a smile. "Now, go enjoy your childhood home. Find a cute boy to hook up with. I hear they make them cute in Austin."

"Are men all you think about, Kristine?" I asked.

"Duh," she said. "Of course not, I also obsess over food." We both laughed and hugged again before I turned to go into the terminal.

"See you in a couple of weeks, beautiful," I said over my shoulder before the sliding doors closed behind me.

When I exited the terminal in Austin to meet my parents, a yelling horde greeted me. Not only were my parents there but also Janice, and my sister, Trish. They all pulled me into a group hug. When they let me breathe again, my dad reached over, took my luggage, and threw it into the back of their Explorer.

"Hop in the middle," Trish said. "That way we can all harass you."

"Sure, thing, sis. While I'm doing that, why don't you fill me in on that new guy you are dating," I said with a mischievous grin.

My sister gave me an evil glare, and then said, "Oh, he is nothing compared to yours. Bringing home the goods to meet the parents, huh?" She punctuated the last word, letting me know I was on the spot this time. Her expression changed, though, when she saw the sadness on my face.

"Martin, what happened?" she asked.

I shook my head. "I'll tell you when we are in the car. No one's coming to meet the parents."

We all loaded into the SUV. Janice put her arm around me and encouraged me to tell what was happening. After I told everyone about the events that morning, the entire vehicle full of people was quiet.

Finally, my dad said, "Son, I know you're angry with this kid, but I for one am glad he decked the other guy in the face. I would have had to go kill him if he had laid a hand on you, and your mom and I already got plans for next week."

I put my hand on my dad's shoulder. "I'm sure you would have, Dad, but I didn't need to be pulled into another family drama. It seems I have a knack for finding those."

My mom chimed in and said, "Well, honey, if you are in the middle of a breakup, I declare we must stop by Billie's Ice Cream Stand and grab some breakup ice cream on the way in." All the occupants of the SUV cheered, including me.

Long ago, Mom had decided ice cream was the only way to cure a broken heart, and if either my sister or I had issues with a love interest, we always ended up at Billie's Ice Cream Stand. The tradition had become so synonymous with breaking up, my sister and I often teased each other about needing to go see Billie when we'd had a bad date or when a love interest didn't share our feelings.

The ice cream was amazing, as usual. Mom always ordered for us when we were broken-hearted, and the recipe for heartache was always the same: two scoops—one chocolate, one vanilla—sitting on top of a brownie and coated with every version of chocolate sprinkle, syrup, hot fudge, and lavished with whipped cream. She would send the concoction back until the whipped cream was so high that the poor kid serving us had to balance it precariously to get it out of the service window.

Basically, breakup ice cream meant if it didn't scrape the bottom of the window when they brought it out, it didn't have enough whipped cream.

Damn, I missed my family. Janice was being really quiet, which meant she was up to something or had something serious to tell me.

Of course, I couldn't finish the ice cream behemoth. I never could, but I did my very best. As always, I felt guilty throwing it away, so I snuck beside the building where the kids at the window couldn't see me and tossed the remainder into the dumpster.

When I came back around, Trish was smiling at me. "You were always afraid of the kids working here. What were they going to do, give you a mean look?"

"I don't know," I said with a smile. "I just thought, after Mom scared them half to death, forcing them to put every ounce of whipped cream in the place on my sundae, that I should've eaten it."

"I don't think they give a damn," she said, laughing at me. Then, she put her arms around my neck. "I'm sorry, brother. I was really hoping you'd met the right one this time."

"Yeah, me too. I kinda thought I had." As we hugged, I said, "He was so fucking hot, Trish. SO FUCKING HOT!"

She pulled back, took my hand, and drew me away from my parents, and we both almost fell down the hill beside the parking lot from giggling so hard.

"Maybe you can make him do penance or something, especially if he was that hot!"

"You have no idea," I told her, "but no, there is no future there. I won't get into a family mixup again. I think the only man I'm willing to date from now on has to be an orphan."

"Little orphan, Big Pete," my sister said, sending us both into another fit of laughter.

When we joined back up with our parents and Janice, everyone had finished their ice cream and was ready to go. I reached over, linked my arm with Janice's and asked, "You gonna tell me what's going on?"

She stiffened in surprise. I could see she was thinking about denying it, but she sighed instead.

"Damn, you could always read me like a book. That sucks, Martin, it really does! Thank God I never have to face you in court. If people could read me like you do, I'd never win a case."

I put my arm around her shoulder and asked her again what was up. "I'll tell you tomorrow when you take me out to breakfast," she said with a sigh. "I do have to tell you something, but I want it to be when we are alone."

I agreed, and we all piled back into my parents' SUV. On the way back to my parents' house, Janice's phone kept dinging, which she ignored.

"Are you going to look at that?" I asked.

"I'm absolutely *not* going to look at anything right now," she said, and her expression halted any other questions.

When we got back to the house, I hugged Janice goodbye, and she agreed to pick me up early. I was exhausted, so I hugged my parents goodnight, telling them I was worn out from this morning's insanity.

Before I went upstairs, I turned around and said to them, "I know y'all are worried, and I appreciate you not asking more questions, but you might as well go search for my name on Google and watch the video. It is going viral, so it'll be spreading through Facebook eventually anyway. At least you'll see for yourselves what happened." Before I could turn to go, my dad stepped up to me and pulled me into a hug. Then, he whispered where my mom couldn't hear.

"I know your mom thinks ice cream is the cure, but it's really whiskey. I have plenty stashed in the garage. When you are ready, you let me know." He hugged me again and winked as he walked into the living room.

I had to be the luckiest man alive to have parents like John and Alicia Williams. They loved us unconditionally and nothing or no one would ever get in the way of them and their kids. I appreciated their love with every ounce of my being.

After Trish went to college, my parents had the house remodeled with the intention of turning it into a bed and breakfast. They'd put jacuzzi tubs in all four bedrooms. Tonight, I had every intention of using that to work out some of the taut nerves. I wished I'd talked Dad into letting me have a bottle of the whiskey he'd told me about, but there was no use getting drunk tonight. Facing Janice was going to be a beast tomorrow. She was the only one here who'd met Elian, and I knew she liked him.

I also knew she'd always be my most fierce defender but that didn't mean she would put up with my bullshit either, and I was beginning to wonder if maybe I'd gone too far telling Elian I never wanted to see him again. Maybe I should've been a little less dramatic. *Shit, no use second-guessing myself now,* I thought. *What was done was done.* There was no way in fucking hell Elian's family would ever tolerate an outsider who'd written the kind of review against one of their own the way I had. No, even if I'd overreacted with Elian, I'd done right by ending it. That much I was sure of.

The jacuzzi was just what the doctor ordered. After my bath, I crawled into bed and fell into a better sleep than I'd anticipated. I woke more refreshed than I should have been the next morning and was up and ready to meet Janice.

When she arrived, she looked a great deal worse than I did. "What the hell is wrong with you?" I asked.

Before I knew it, she was bawling her eyes out. "Oh my God, Martin, I fell in love, and I've fucked it up. I'm going to be alone forever."

Well, I thought to myself, *this is certainly the shoe on the other foot.*

"Honey, it's probably not that bad. Tell me what happened," I said.

We sat down at my parents' kitchen table, and she told me about a guy she'd met. "We were being flirty and taking it easy until I went into a bar with one of my girlfriends and found the son of a bitch with another woman.

"I went off my rocker. I know we didn't have an exclusive relationship, but all I could see was red. So, I went up to him and punched him in the arm really hard. In fact, so hard I think I dislocated my finger."

She glanced down at her hand, which was a little swollen.

"So, what did he say?" I asked.

"He was livid. He asked what the hell I did that for, and then I pointed at the gorgeous blonde and said, 'Because of her!' Then, I turned around in my most practiced diva twirl and proceeded to walk off.

Unfortunately, I didn't even get two steps before he grabbed me by the arm and flipped me around."

At this point, Janice had begun to cry again. "When I was facing him, the bastard pointed to the gorgeous blonde and said, 'Janice, meet my sister Beth.'" I was so angry I couldn't just let it go, and I yelled, 'Yeah, right, you fucking two-timer,' and tried to leave again. But he embraced me again and pointed at the woman and told her to show me her hand, which she did, and there was a wedding ring on it. I should have quit yelling and smiled or done something proper, like a real Southern woman would know how to do, but instead, I accused him of dating a married woman. When I did that, his face turned bright red, and he literally screamed at me, 'She is fucking pregnant!'

"When I looked closer that time, I could see he was right. Then, I noticed they both had the same smile, Martin. The same fucking smile!" She burst into tears again and shook her head. "I just ran after that. I'm so embarrassed."

"Is he the one who kept dinging you last night?" I asked.

She sighed, then said, "Yes, this all happened before I met your parents to pick you up. I was having drinks with my girlfriend from work when I saw them. He's been texting since I ran off."

"You haven't texted him back?" I asked, a bit shocked.

"Have you texted the Cuban back?" she asked with attitude.

"He hasn't texted me," I sighed.

"Oh, honey," Janice said and jumped up to put her arms around me.

"We are a couple of fucking ninnies," she said. "Let's go drown our sorrows in a Texas-sized breakfast *with* mimosas."

"God, that sounds perfect," I replied, and we headed downtown toward our favorite little breakfast place.

We commiserated about our recent bad experiences with men. I showed the video to Janice, and I could tell she was having to work overtime not to laugh about it.

"He really hit that asshole right in the face, didn't he?" she asked.

"Do *not* take his side, Janice. That asshole is his cousin, and you and I both know how things end up when I get in the middle of family issues."

"Shit, you are right," she said. "No matter how hot that was, it was still not cool."

"You've had too many mimosas," I chided.

"No, I have not," she proclaimed a little too loudly, then sunk into her seat. "Okay, time to switch to coffee."

"No shit, Sherlock," I said with a laugh.

We were both enjoying the morning, laughing about all the crap going on and were about to leave when a hunky, tall, redheaded man came over to where we sat.

"Janice," he said, in what sounded to me like a bit of an Irish brogue. When she heard his voice, her head came up and all the blood drained from her face.

I was mesmerized. In all the time I'd known this woman, I'd never known her to be so affected by a guy. The man reached around her, grabbed my hand, and shook it.

"Hi, I'm Kevin," he said. "I'm Janice's boyfriend." Then, he gave me a cold hard look that said he could snap me in two.

"I'm Martin, and I'm Janice's best friend from high school, college, and when she screws up with her boyfriend."

Janice kicked me hard under the table. "Ouch," I said. "Damn, Janice, I still have to use that leg, you know!"

"Fuck you, Martin," she replied, then turned her anger on Kevin. "Why are you here?"

"Because you won't answer my calls or my texts, and I know this is where you go on Saturday mornings. So, I decided to come here to see you whether you wanted to see me or not."

He seemed to run out of breath, trying to get everything he could say in one sentence, assuming Janice wouldn't give him a chance to speak again.

"I don't want to see you, Kevin," she said.

"Why, because I was having lunch with my sister?"

"No," she said, "because I'm a fucking idiot. Martin, can we go?"

Before I could get up, Kevin had lifted Janice to her feet and planted a huge kiss on her. Several people in seats next to us applauded while the rest watched with ever-increasing curiosity.

When Janice resurfaced from the kiss, her face was flushed, and her lips had formed a smile. "I don't care if you're embarrassed," Kevin told her. "I loved that you were jealous and were willing to fight for me. You also impressed my sister, who said I would be an idiot to let a fire sprite like you get away." Janice's face turned another shade of crimson at the mention of his sister. "My family is demanding that I bring you to lunch tomorrow so they can get to know you."

Janice shook her head. "I couldn't possibly do that. They will all hate me."

Kevin shook his head. "They adore you and totally think it's a good omen that you put a bruise on my arm because you thought I was flirting with another woman."

He lifted his sleeve and showed me a very impressive bruise that seemed to match the level of a punch that would cause Janice's finger to swell as it had. "You couldn't have impressed my sister more if you'd have shown up with a leprechaun on your shoulder."

Janice smiled, then turned to me. I was doing everything in my power to resist laughing at the situation. Luckily, she burst into laughter for me.

"I'm an idiot, Kevin, but if you'll still have me, I'd love to go meet your family" she said, and then blushed again.

I shook my head. Janice had to be all in with this one. Not only had this man disarmed her and caused her to lose her cool, but he also caused her to blush repeatedly. The thing that shocked me to no end was this guy had convinced her to meet his parents after an embarrassing event. None of that sounded like my cool, collected, and often harsh girlfriend, Janice. *Good for her*, I thought. *Even better for Kevin.* I grinned as the two kissed again.

I stood to go to the restroom, allowing Kevin to take my seat. I already knew my morning with Janice was over, so on my way to the restroom, I ordered a cab. When I came out, the two were moonie-eyed over each other and had all but forgotten I existed.

I went up and told them I'd ordered a cab and would see Janice later. She grabbed my hand before I could go. "Kevin has to go to a gala at this firm tomorrow night and asked me to be his date, which I agreed to before... *yesterday*." She put her hand over her mouth as she said the word. "I want to spend time with you, but I promised Kevin..."

She waved at him as she spoke. "He will have to pop around and be social, and I don't want to sit by myself. Please come," she begged. "We can sit and make fun of everyone's clothing options and the bad catering."

"Hey," Kevin said. "I oversaw the catering."

"Oh, honey, I'm sorry," she said. "We'll only make fun of it when you aren't around then." Kevin rolled his eyes as Janice leaned over and kissed him.

"I'll check with Mom and Dad to see what plans they have for tomorrow night. Then I'll text you," I said.

Janice stood up, hugged me, and whispered, "Thanks for letting me play hookey from our play date. I think I need to have makeup sex with this handsome man before he decides to dump me after all."

I glanced over at Kevin and smiled. "That sounds like a great idea." Then, I winked at the unsuspecting man.

As I walked out, Kevin continued to watch me with a perplexed expression. I could tell he was concerned about what Janice and I had plotted, but I was almost totally sure he wouldn't mind the outcome she had planned.

When the cab dropped me off at my parents', I walked in to find them sitting in the living room, both snoring while the TV had some old Western playing in the background.

I chuckled at them, climbed the stairs to my old room, and pulled my laptop out, sitting back on the bed. I watched the stupid video again and poured through the comments, trying to figure out how much damage to my reputation and to the paper this little episode would have.

There are always trolls, but there were fewer than I thought there'd be. Most of the comments were positive, and even most of the usual trolls were impressed by how valiant Elian had been. In fact, most of the comments were about him, and I'd been more of a backdrop in the discussion. That was good at least. If the story centered more on me and less on Elian, it would have been a bigger firestorm for the paper, whether I was cast in a good *or* bad light.

Then, I switched over to the newspaper blog, and things had improved dramatically there. Almost every comment was positive and encouraging. Thousands of comments had come through the blog, most of them thanking the paper for bringing out the nasty conditions the restaurant had exposed them to. I was surprised there was no mention of the video, but I guessed the video crowd was unlikely to be folks that followed the paper's blog.

I shut my computer and grabbed my phone to text Kristine.

There was a text from Elian, and it simply read, "I'm so sorry, Martin. I miss you so much." That was all.

As tears came to my eyes, I decided to delete the text instead of leaving it on my phone, afraid it'd entice me to answer.

Before I was done, I'd deleted Elian's number altogether. Of course, I just laughed at myself because

Elian's was one of the few numbers I had memorized. However, the act of deleting it confirmed for me how important it was for me not to let my feelings cloud my judgment.

I closed my eyes and saw Peter's mother with her lips pressed into a frown, the way she got every time she finished calling me names. I wasn't going to let that be a repeated event. *No, it is better to let this end here before things got uglier,* I thought.

I texted Kristine, "I just went through the blog and the website, and it appears like the paper and I are going to get off easy."

She responded back, "Yep, sales this week have risen over five percent. Congrats, you will be the poster boy here when you get back."

"Seriously doubt that will keep the board from discussing cutting my position again by this time next week, though."

She texted back after a few minutes, "Probably, but if you were off the chopping block for a week, you accomplished something!"

"Truth," I texted back.

A few minutes later, Kristine texted again, "You doing okay, sweetie?"

"No, not really, but I'm surviving. I really needed family. You were right on the money with that suggestion!"

"I know, honey. We miss you, though," she said.

"I miss you, too," I replied and put my phone down. I was going to lie down when I heard a knock on the door.

"Martin, it's Mom. Can I come in?" she asked.

"Yeah, sure," I said.

My mom walked in, smiling. "You slipped out early this morning. We felt bad that we didn't see you before you left."

I glanced over at her and asked, "Yeah, what's up with that? You used to be up with the birds."

"Oh," she chuckled with embarrassment, "we love being retired. We stay up late playing cards or watching TV or whatever." Then, there was a blush on her face. "We aren't used to getting up until after ten or eleven these days."

"That's good, I guess." I smiled, trying not to think of the *whatever*. "Janice needed to talk, so we slipped out early."

"Where is Janice?" Mom asked. "I assumed she'd be around all day."

"Oh, well, some hunky Irishman came and took her away from me."

"Really?" Mom lit up at the prospect of a juicy story.

"He came in and swept her off her feet, and glared at me like he could rip me in half. Then, he convinced her to go visit his parents tomorrow," I concluded with a smile.

"Well, we'll have to invite that man and Janice over this week, so I can get a good look at him."

"I'll ask them," I said. "Speaking of that, they asked me to go with them tomorrow night to one of his firm's gala events. Do y'all have plans for us?"

"No, honey, we didn't even expect you until Monday. We will be home being our boring selves. Go on out and have fun."

I smiled. "I hope to have a lot of boring nights with you two." Then, I leaned over and kissed her on the cheek. "Thanks for rescuing me again, Mom. I really didn't intend to need it again."

"Oh, sweetheart, love is a chess match. You play your best until some old queen boots you off the board."

I turned to my mother in surprise. "You've been saving that, haven't you?"

"I have," she said with pride. "It seemed perfect right then."

"You are the perfect mom," I said as I hugged her.

"Aaah," she said and hugged me back. "Come down in a bit. I think your dad wants to get you drunk in the garage before he takes you for a ride in the Hill Country."

"You know about his stash?" I asked.

"Son, I know everything that happens in this house, but don't you let your dad know that. As long as he thinks he has that hidden in the hole below the floor, he will be able to hold onto that rebellious streak I love so much about him." Then, she giggled and closed the door behind her.

I wondered why I couldn't find a love like my parents'. Not that they didn't fight. I'd heard them have some major blowouts over the years, but I never saw them go to bed angry, and they always worked through their anger, no matter what the issue was. What was always present in my parents' relationship was love, respect, and compassion. What impressed me the most—and the thing I wanted for myself—was that both of them were the other person's *one*. When push came to shove, they stood like a pillar of strength for each other. That was what had been missing in all my relationships. No one seemed to see me as their *one*, as the person they put above all other people.

I knew unless I had that- which was probably a fantasy- I'd never be content with anyone. I was probably doomed to be alone for the rest of my life.

***

I was ready to go before Janice and Kevin came to pick me up. I wore a suit of mine from high school that, luckily, still fit me. In fact, I was pleased to see I filled out the ass a lot better now.

I was feeling confident about the outfit when I walked downstairs, and both my parents whistled.

"Okay, you are embarrassing me," I said, fussing at them.

"You are looking good, son," Dad said.

"Thanks, Dad. Who knows? I might meet the man of my dreams tonight, and when we are old and gray, I can tell the story of how I netted him with the suit I wore to my high school formal dance."

"That'll be quite a story, honey," my mother chuckled.

When Janice and Kevin finally showed up, they quickly bustled me into the car. Kevin was afraid he was going to be late and—like he already told us—he was in charge of catering. If anything was coming apart, he needed to be there to help manage it.

The gala was being held at the iconic Long Center for the Performing Arts. As we entered the building, I thought this was the perfect place for an architectural firm to hold a gala. Kevin took Janice around to introduce her to the firm's leadership, then left her with me to go check on the catering.

"So, how did the family event go?" I asked with a chuckle.

"Oh my God, Martin. I love his family." Suddenly, she looked at me with concern and said, "I'm sorry, that was insensitive."

"No, it wasn't," I assured her. "It is my curse to deal with momzillas and cousins from hell, not yours."

I leaned over to her and kissed her cheek. "I'm so happy for you. Now, give me the juice. What did the sister say when you showed up?"

"Believe it or not, his sister came over, grabbed me in a huge bear hug, and told me she was so happy that her Kevin had found a woman who won't let him get away with shit. I guess his ex-girlfriend was some kind of jellyfish that grated the nerves of the steely women in his family."

I chuckled and said, "Well, that won't be a problem with you now, will it?"

Janice playfully punched my arm. "Be nice to me," she whined. "It was tough meeting his parents, but it may be tougher now that I kinda like them. It isn't every day you meet a group of women who aren't on the warpath to destroy any other woman who comes into their territory. That whole family seemed to put their arms around me and embrace me. Then, when you top that with the hunk of a man they have created, it's hard not to want to be a part of the whole package."

Grinning at her, I asked, "Have you told him you love him yet?" Janice glared back at me in shock as her color shifted to a shade of light green.

"No, Martin. Why would you ask that?" she asked, trying to hide her discomfort.

"Because, baby, I've known you most of my life, and you have never been this gaga over a man before. How long have you two been dating anyway?" I asked.

"Since last year. But Martin, until I almost broke his arm—or more accurately, my fingers—we hadn't even discussed being exclusive. That was my hang-up, Martin, not his."

"I know, honey, but here's the thing, if he didn't have feelings for you, he wouldn't have taken you to his parents' house."

I thought for a moment. Realizing in my head that I was projecting my own crap onto the situation, I added, "Unless the fucker is screwed up and insane."

Janice cocked her eyebrow at me. "Yeah, that was fucked up. I'm sorry you had to go through all that," she said, acknowledging she realized I was thinking about my first and second dates with Elian. "Have you heard from the fucker?"

"Yeah, he texted yesterday, but I ignored it. In fact, I deleted him completely out of my phone. I was feeling empowered." I shrugged when she gave me a skeptical look.

"Deleting him from your phone isn't the same as your heart," she said. "Trust me, I'm an expert on this topic."

I nodded my agreement. "I know, but for tonight, he is deleted, and I'm here with my girlfriend and her very hot boyfriend, whom she has fallen in love with... although she hasn't told him yet." This earned me my second arm punch of the evening.

"Now, are we going to sit in an inconspicuous place and bash the party guests and the food like you promised or not?" I asked, causing her to laugh.

We had just stood up when someone tapped me on the shoulder. "Martin?" a voice asked. I turned around, and the world dropped out from underneath me. Standing in front of me was a spectacularly dressed, too damned fucking hot, Peter Reed.

I froze for a moment before the blood returned to my head. I heard myself stammer and ask, "Pe... Peter, why are you here?"

Peter laughed and had the decency to appear embarrassed. "This firm is recruiting me to join them and move back to Austin. I was invited to come tonight to check out their gala."

Not knowing what else to say, I looked over to Janice for help.

Janice stepped right up and reached for Peter's hand. "Peter, it's been a long time," she said. As she shook his hand, she moved him slightly, so he was facing away from me. "So, you are thinking about moving back to Austin then? That's good."

I took the moment to collect my thoughts and get myself together as my friend, thankfully, took over the conversation.

After getting my bearings, I realized I really didn't want to talk to Peter. I decided the best thing to do was end the conversation in a way that made my reluctance clear but in a way that would also be respectful and appropriate for the situation.

"Peter, it's nice to see you. I hope all is well, but Janice and I have a date over at the bar. You have a great night and good luck on your new position," I said and grabbed Janice's arm, pulling her toward the bar.

"Smooth," Janice replied as we walked away.

"I've learned how to forcefully, yet tactfully excuse myself from an unwanted discussion. It is a very necessary skill in my industry," I replied after a laugh.

"Well, I'd have given a lot of money to capture Peter's expression on camera," she joked.

I laughed. "He definitely hasn't met confident Martin before. I'm a little different from when we dated. It doesn't really matter, though, what he thinks."

Janice stopped and turned to me. "I can't tell you how happy I am to hear that. He never deserved you, Martin, especially if he was willing to throw you away like he did."

"That's the damned truth," I agreed. When we sat down at the bar, I ordered two shots of tequila, which

I downed immediately. As I sighed from the hit, I turned to Janice, just as her eyes were growing wider.

"Martin, he's coming back."

"Oh, shit," I said. "I guess he didn't get the hint."

"Clearly not," she said as he came back up to us.

"Martin, I'm sorry. Can I have a moment to speak with you? I promise it won't take long."

"No, Peter," I remarked without pausing. "We have nothing to say to one another. Shit, man, it has been two years. If I had known you would be here, I wouldn't have come." As confidently as I could, I added, "If you don't mind, Peter, I'm here with Janice and her boyfriend, and I would really like to enjoy the evening. That can't happen if you keep coming into my space. I mean no disrespect, but please go away."

This was all said quietly and in a way that no one but Janice and Peter could hear. Peter's face fell, and without another comment, he walked away and disappeared into the crowd.

"Well, isn't that some shit?" I said with a sigh.

"That is some major shit," Janice agreed. She waved to the bartender and ordered four more shots.

When they arrived, she downed two, and I downed the others.

"This is going to be an interesting night," I said to no one in particular.

Peter had effectively disappeared and neither Janice nor I caught sight of him again. I assumed he must have gone home with his tail between his legs. Peter had never been good with confrontation and tended to blow his stack, then regret it. His leaving was probably the best for me *and* his potential career with this firm.

Despite Peter's appearance and strange request to talk, the rest of the evening was fun. Janice, Kevin, and I danced with other couples. We drank, laughed a lot, and thoroughly enjoyed the event.

As we rode home together, I congratulated Kevin on the affair. "Those things are usually stuffy and boring, but your firm did a good job making it fun and light-hearted. Even the food was great, which is a feat when it comes to catering one of those. Who did you use?" When he told me Auburn Top Catering, I smiled.

"I'm glad they've made it. They were tiny when I was here, but they had great potential. I had a feeling, if they got their feet under them, they'd do well."

We talked and laughed on the way back to my parents' house, and when they dropped me off, it was well past one in the morning. "I almost feel like I'm sneaking back after curfew," I joked.

"It isn't like we haven't done that before," Janice joked back.

"Shh, my parents don't need to know anything about that!" I giggled as I got out of the car.

"I love you, Janice Girl," I said, leaning back into the car to give her a smooch. "Kevin, you better treat her like a queen tonight, and I'm not talking about the royal kind."

"I have plans to do that very thing," Kevin said with a mischievous expression on his face.

I wiggled my eyebrows at Janice, and she blushed appropriately. *Again, with the blushing*, I thought. I wondered how long it would be before the wedding bells chimed. "You kids have fun," I said as they drove off.

I went into the house thinking it would be locked up, only to find my parents sitting at the table in a full-out war about some rule my mother said my dad had broken. There were cards on the table, and Mom was standing with her hands on her hips.

"Mom, Dad, what's going on?" I asked.

"Oh, hi, honey," my mom replied. "It is nothing. Your dad is trying to cheat again."

"You mean, you are trying to make up new rules to the game," Dad replied.

"Well, I see you two are getting along, so I'll just go up to bed," I said, shaking my head.

"No, honey, don't go. Sit with us for a minute and tell us about the evening," Mom said. "Besides, we are at a stalemate anyway." She looked over at her husband and winked at him. "I'll take care of you later," she warned. The way she said that made my face turn red.

Mom went into the kitchen and hollered out to me, "Can I get you something? Do you want a beer or juice?

"I should probably drink some water if I want to avoid a hangover."

"Good idea," Mom added and brought me two glasses of water, placing them in front of me.

"You'll never guess who showed up tonight," I said.

Both parents looked at me blankly. When I said, "Peter," however, their expressions quickly changed from blank to anger.

"What the hell?" Dad said. "Did Janice know that jackass was going to be there?"

"No, none of us knew. He was being recruited by the firm. He just showed up."

"What did he say to you?" Mom asked.

"He wanted to talk to me alone."

Dad stood up as he asked, "Did you?"

"No, I basically told him to get lost and luckily, he did."

"I'll be damned," Dad said. "The boy has some balls, doesn't he?"

"I know him," I said. "If he has it in his brain that we need to talk, he'll probably show up here. I just wanted you two to be prepared to see him."

"Want me to break his nose?" Dad asked, a sly grin slowly crossing his face.

"As much as I'd like to say yeah, I've already had someone face-punch a guy for me this week. I'd rather avoid that, if possible."

"Damn, Martin, you are no fun," Dad said, and Mom put her hand over his.

"Well, honey, if you don't want a guy to punch him, I could do it for you."

Despite the serious situation, both Dad and I burst out laughing at the image of my sweet mother hitting anyone in the face.

"What?" she asked. "You don't think I can't hit that son of a bitch in the face? After he hurt my baby like he did? I could put him in the hospital!"

"Honey, of course, we know you can kick his ass!" Dad reached over and kissed his wife squarely on the mouth. "Just when I think I couldn't be more in love with you," he said and kissed her again.

"What do you want us to do if he shows up, Martin?" Mom asked. Then, after she thought a moment, she said, "I won't promise to be nice to the SOB, but I can promise neither your father nor I will hit him. At least, not in reality, although I don't promise I won't be *imagining* him writhing in pain at my feet."

I couldn't help but smile at my parents. They always had my back, and that mattered more and more every day. "If he comes," I said, "then I'll go talk to him and put an end to the nonsense. I guess it'd be nice to get some closure. I haven't spoken to him since that day. It still seems so surreal how we were engaged one minute and separated the next, never to speak again."

"He is deranged, honey, just like his mother. You can't fix people like that. You just have to deal with them."

"And," Dad added, "you thank the good Lord you didn't marry him."

"Ain't that the truth," I agreed.

I hugged them both then and headed up to bed.

The next morning, I was up before my parents. I'd put a pot of coffee on when the doorbell rang. I looked at the clock and rolled my eyes. "Peter," I said to myself. Sure enough, when I opened the door, there stood my ex.

Peter didn't appear to have slept the night before. I didn't invite him in, but rather went outside and gestured for him to sit on the porch swing while I sat in a rocking chair next to it. "What do you want, Peter?" I asked.

"I needed to see you," Peter began.

"No, you didn't," I said to stop him before he went on. "This isn't going to be a storybook reunion, Peter, so you can cut out the sappy bullshit. You said you wanted to speak to me, so speak. I'm sitting right here... at least for another minute."

Peter sighed. "I guess you aren't going to forgive me, huh?"

"I forgave you a long time ago, but I sure as hell don't want to spend time with you. Again, what is it you have on your mind that after two years of not speaking, you need to talk to me about now?"

"Give me a minute, Martin, please. This is hard to do," he replied.

Peter took a breath and let it out slowly and said, "I fucked up with you, and I've regretted it for almost as long as we've been broken up. I tried to date other men, but I can only think of you. When I saw you last night, I thought it might be providence, that maybe this would be my chance to make up for what happened, and maybe we could have another chance."

"Buddy," I began, "if you came here thinking you were going to get back with me, you are barking up the wrong tree. There will never be another chance for us. Hell, man, I don't think there could be a chance that we'd ever be friends, much less lovers."

I stood to leave, and Peter jumped up. "Wait! I need to explain things to you... what happened back then. I think it'll help you understand it."

I sat down, put my hands in my lap, and waited for Peter to explain. Peter sat back down, too, and wiped his hand over his face.

"My mom was a bitch to you. Shortly after we broke up..." he started, then looking over at me, corrected himself. "When I broke up with you, Mom ended up in the hospital with a tumor. The doctors confirmed the tumor is what caused her to say such nasty things. I knew it was uncharacteristic. I think that's why I didn't believe you.

"After the surgery, she was racked with guilt and told me in detail what she had said to you. I tried to reach you but you'd blocked me on social media. When I came here to tell you in person, your parents told me you'd moved out of state."

Peter rubbed his eyes and sighed. "Shortly after that, I got my assignment in Georgia. Your parents wouldn't tell me where you'd gone and it didn't feel right to stalk you so I didn't reach out to you. When I saw you last night, Martin, I couldn't help but come here and talk to you. I still think about you almost every day. You were the one that got away."

The anger had gone out of me, and I sat rocking in the chair while listening to Peter explain. "I'm glad you explained what happened. Mom and Dad told me you'd stopped by and that you told them your mom had a brain tumor, but it didn't really make much sense. I did look it up and found the type she had. So yeah, it's plausible. I'm happy she is okay," I said.

"I know she'd like to see you... to apologize," Peter said.

"Yeah, tumor or not, that ain't going to happen, Peter. It took me a long time to get myself pulled together after you and your mom ripped me apart. I chalked it up to being too young to handle adult relationships, but I'm still having to learn to trust again because of all that."

Peter sighed, and his longing was clearly apparent in his eyes. "We were both young, and I was stupid. Now that you know Mom's reaction to you was medical and not personal, you still don't think we could start again?"

I closed my eyes and rocked in the chair. I wanted to be able to put closure on this for myself, and now for Peter, too. When I opened my eyes, I leaned forward in the rocker and grabbed Peter's hand in my own.

"Peter, I loved you. I guess part of me will always love you, but no, there is never going to be another us. That part of my life is over, and after you shut the door, my wounds finally began to heal. I never want to reopen it again, Peter. I don't want to be in a relationship with you."

I sighed, seeing the hurt and confusion in Peter's face as I went on. "It's good that your mom wasn't just hateful because she didn't like me, but that doesn't change your reaction. No matter what we'd do to try to mend this relationship, I would always know that when push came to shove, you chose not to believe me."

When Peter opened his mouth to argue, I put my hand up and added, "I know you should choose family first, but you chose her before you even knew what had happened. You assumed I, your fiancé, was lying before you had a chance to ask her if I wasn't. You can't change that. For me, that means no matter what, I'd always be second best to you, and worse, I'd always be waiting for you to let me down again. Even if you swore you were different or that you'd changed. I can't be my husband's second, Peter. If I can't be your primary person, then I can't be your husband."

I could see the light finally coming on for Peter. Before I knew it, Peter had me in an embrace.

"I will always love you, too, Martin, and as much as it hurts to admit it, I can see you're right. It's time to move on."

I nodded, not trusting my emotions wouldn't betray me. I watched Peter walk out to his car parked on the street, and then pull away. As soon as he was out of sight, the tears spilled over, and I sat back on the chair, pulled my knees up to my chest, and let them flow.

Within moments, Mom, Dad, and Trish were on the porch. My sister knelt next to me with her head on my leg, with Mom and Dad standing on either side, a hand on each of my shoulders.

"So, I guess you heard all that," I said.

They all three nodded but didn't say anything, just kept their hands on me.

"It's not that I'm crying because I miss him or want him back but because, if he had found me after his mom's surgery, I probably would've forgiven him. Truth is, I've wanted him back all this time. For two years, I waited for him to come back."

I let another wave of tears overwhelm me. "I didn't realize until now that I'd never really been able to get over the fact he dumped me before he had all the facts. That wouldn't change, and I would always be waiting for him to hurt me again. I didn't get that until just now."

The tears continued to flow when Dad reached down and kissed me on the head. "You are one of the bravest men I've ever met. Right now, you are my hero, son." Of course, this just made the waterworks flow harder.

After a few minutes, I said, "Okay, I think we've made enough of a show for the neighbors on a Monday morning. Mom, do you have champagne? I'm suddenly having a strong desire for mimosas, and we can celebrate me closing an important chapter of my life."

The family went in, and Mom whirled through the kitchen like the old days, whipping up a large breakfast. Trish poured orange juice, and I poured champagne. She was still too young to drink, but that didn't stop her from giving me the stink eye when I obviously omitted pouring champagne into her glass.

Dad snuck out to the garage and brought in some Jack, placing it on the table and said, "In case you need something a little stronger, son." Mom shot Dad a nasty look but didn't say anything about the whiskey.

The rest of the day was perfect. Trish had to work, so she left shortly after breakfast. I joined my parents in several hands of poker, which switched to spades when my sister got home. That was better anyway since my parents ended up nose to nose repeatedly over rules regarding the different card games.

"You both know you could find the rules on Google, right?" I asked.

"Now, what would be the fun in that?" my mother asked and winked at me.

Despite the drama related to my arrival and Peter's visit, the rest of my stay in Austin was uneventful. I hung out with old friends, and visited Hippie Hollow, my favorite watering hole, where people came to swim naked. I also went fishing with my dad, went into town to watch the bats fly out from under the Congress Bridge, and had one of the most relaxing vacations I'd had in some time.

By the time the second week was ending, though, I was hungry for my life back in Fort Lauderdale. I'd decided not to text Kristine about Peter. She was already worried about me, but I also wanted to fill her in on the drama in person, knowing how much she liked that kind of thing.

When Sunday finally arrived, my parents drove me to the airport. My mom cried about me leaving, which was her usual M.O. Dad also looked forlorn, and both my parents told me how much they loved me and would miss me. Once again, I remembered how lucky I was to have them.

Kristine met me at the airport when I arrived back in Fort Lauderdale. She was bursting at the seams to tell me all about the happenings since I'd been gone.

The biggest thing was that the Cuban restaurant had closed and there was a for-sale sign on the window.

"That didn't take long." I sighed.

"Well, the death knell was the video. The entire city went up in arms when that came out, and it appears you are now our little celebrity," she said enthusiastically.

"No more anonymous reviews, I guess," I replied regrettably.

"That's seriously doubtful," she said. "No matter, your reviews will be coveted, so when there is something new, everyone will look to you for direction."

"I feel like I've become the stereotypical old gay restaurant guy," I said with as much distaste as I could.

Kristine peered over at me quizzically. "I thought you'd be happy about this. What's crawled up in you?"

"I am happy, Kristine. I'm just bummed about how things came down with Elian," I said with a sigh.

"Aaah, you miss him," she said.

I nodded. "It doesn't matter if I miss him or not. It's over. If his cousin hadn't ended it, I certainly did when I ignored his texts."

"He texted you?" Kristine asked, shocked. "You never told me he tried to reach you again."

"He did, and I ignored him. I even deleted his name and info out of my phone. I thought I was done with him." I sighed again.

"Well, if you miss him and want to see him again, then you need to give him a call sooner than later," she said. "You know that man is beyond hot after he heroically belted his cousin in the nose for you. I'm sure every eligible man in the city is after him."

"No, it's over," I said. "Even if I chased him down, and he took me back, his family would disown him for coming after me. They are all really close, Kristine. Blood is thicker than water. Even if that water is boiling hot."

Kristine laughed. "I think you're wrong. Families fight all the time, and when a man stands up to them to defend his love, families tend to respect that. Besides, you could both move to California or something and leave them all here."

I turned toward Kristine, who was now merging into traffic and asked, "You would be okay with that?"

She jerked and almost stepped on the brakes before thinking better of it. "Forget that. I was in friend mode, not editor mode. You may *never* move to California. But I'd be willing to help you kidnap them and ship all of them there." She glanced over at me and winked.

As we drove, I filled her in on seeing Peter in Austin, which almost caused her to do another full stop. Luckily, she had her wits about her today, and we made it safely to my apartment.

She dropped me off after I'd told her I was too tired to hang out. The truth was I didn't want to talk about Elian *or* Peter anymore. I was tired of men and wanted to sit in my tub, drink a lot of chardonnay, and relax. Since a week ago, I'd decided I wanted to do a follow-up article or blog about the big deal with the restaurant closing, and I hadn't been able to get my mind wrapped around it.

I guessed I needed to talk to Elian at some point and get his take on the events since he was now a big part of it all. Anyone who read the article or saw the video would be curious how everything played out with him.

The thought of seeing Elian both excited and scared the crap out of me. The last thing I told him was I never wanted to see him again. That was two weeks ago. The only thing I'd heard from him since then was a text. A text I ignored. The message from me was clear to anyone who was listening: *Martin is a cold, heartless bitch.*

I couldn't imagine Elian would ever be willing to see me again, even if we could make things work with his family, which clearly wasn't ever going to happen.

As I was unpacking my bag, I was surprised to see Dad had stowed away his prized whiskey in my checked luggage. I laughed. My father wasn't overly emotional, but when he saw me hurting, he had no qualms about making sure I was stocked with the "forget-everything potent."

My father was nothing if not a good ol' Southern boy, and in his mind, whiskey could get a man through any problem. At the moment, I wasn't in disagreement. I poured myself three fingers and toasting my absent father, I downed it before going to get that bath.

Luckily, the bath and the whiskey seemed to have the desired effect, and I was asleep before I knew what hit me.

The next morning, I took another cab into work. I still wasn't sure the coast was fully clear, and I'd rather avoid any lurking Alverezes if I could.

I had the driver drop me off in front of the infamous coffee shop, and when I walked in, I got a round of applause from the baristas. I didn't linger long after my order was filled; instead, I rushed to my office. We had a new person at the front desk. Normally, I'd have stopped and introduced myself, but she was on the phone so I waved at her, intending to meet her officially later.

Before I could get past her, however, she quickly put the person she was speaking to on hold and asked if I was going to be in the office all day today.

"That's the plan," I replied and continued back toward my office. I wasn't sure what had prompted the question, especially since I assumed she didn't know me, but the answer became clear about an hour later when the same secretary knocked on my door.

When she came in, she said, "There's an older woman by the name of Bonita Alverez who would like a meeting with you. Are you available, or do you want me to make an appointment for later?"

I was shocked that Elian's aunt, the muscle man's mother, was here.

"Did she say why she's here?" I asked.

"She said she needed to speak to you about a private matter. Should I ask her for more specifics?"

"No, just tell her it'll be a moment."

I slipped out of my office behind the secretary and down to Kristine's. I walked in and closed the door behind me. "This is going to be a problem," I told her.

"What?" Kristine asked, noticing for the first time I was in her office.

"Elian's aunt, the mom of the guy who threatened me, has just shown up. She is out front waiting to see me."

"Oh, shit," Kristine replied.

"Yeah," I agreed.

"Do you want me to meet her with you?"

"No, I think I better do this alone, but I'll keep the door open. Why don't you hang around, though, in case things go bad."

"Yeah, I think that's a good idea."

When I got back to my office, I phoned the secretary, and told her to send Mrs. Alverez back to my office.

"Señora Alverez," I greeted her when she came to my door. "Welcome. Can I get you anything to drink?"

"No, mijo, I'm here for a quick visit. Thank you for seeing me."

The woman took a deep breath and got right down to business. "We all know about this restaurant shit. We are all mad as can be at my son for being so stupid. He embarrassed himself and the family with how he treated you, and my first order of business here is to tell you we, Elian's entire family, want you to know how sorry we are."

"Thank you, señora Alverez," I replied, genuinely surprised.

"Ian, my son... His papa has been trying to get him to go into the condo business with him. And he should because, unlike the restaurant business, he is actually very good at real estate, but his dream was always to own restaurants like his cousin. The truth is, I think he is a little jealous of Elian, and that is what this was all about," she said. She sighed then and finally sat down.

"I can imagine the family got pretty angry when the restaurant had to close and all the negative public stuff came out," I said, feeling the sadness I'd felt the past two weeks settle on me again.

Señora Alverez laughed. "No mijo, we are all relieved someone had the balls to get this ridiculous idea out of his head once and for all." She reached over the desk and put her hand over mine.

"You know, Martin, we love all our children, and we want them to have the very best." She hesitated for a moment, then said, "Since I met you that night on the beach, I knew you were Elian's very best."

When I tried to explain we were no longer together, she just laughed. "You love my nephew," she said, "and he loves you. We all know this. You know this." She took a moment to text someone, which I thought was weird. Then, she said, "But, I will tell you something you don't know. When my son came home, calling you names and threatening to dismember you, he had everyone upset. We all saw the video where Elian hit him in the mouth, and that usually would've put an end to it. As far as I know, Elian has never hit anyone before, and I think Ian was hoping to save face, but when Ian said something threatening about you again, Elian leaped up to your defense."

She chuckled. "Poor Ian was speechless. I'd never seen him like that. You see, Elian is the peacemaker in our family. He never raises his voice. Even so, when he came to your defense in front of the family, I don't think Ian knew how to handle it."

"So, what happened?" I asked, enthralled by the story.

"Ian sat down and shut up." señora Alverez laughed so hard that I couldn't help but catch some of her humor. When she stopped laughing, she said, "Mijo, you have to know Elian would never stand up to his cousin if he didn't care deeply for you." She patted my hand then and smiled.

"Go to Elian. He feels bad about confronting his cousin. At least having the man he loves by his side would make the effort worth it, Martin."

Just as I thought she was going to stand to leave, she announced, "Now, Ian has something he wants to say to you. Then, in a shrill Mom voice, she yelled, "IAN!" To my surprise, a few moments later, the big muscle man walked in.

"Now, Ian, what do you want to say to Mr. Williams?"

It took every ounce of my self-control not to laugh at the expression on Ian's face. The thirty-something -year-old man, who appeared at that moment like he was thirteen again, said, "I'm sorry, Martin."

"For what?" his mother asked.

Ian waited a moment, looked at his mother, and said, "Mama, I need to do this in my own way. Please, give me a moment."

Ian turned toward me then with a different, mature expression on his face.

"Mr. Williams, I have been a shit. I've taken my anger out on you instead of on my staff, who are the ones to blame for your horrible night. Did Elian or Mama tell you why I was so upset?" he asked.

"All she has told me," I admitted, "was that you wanted to compete with your cousin. I haven't seen Elian since that day."

Ian glanced guiltily at his mother, who was sending hateful darts at him.

"You see," Ian continued, "I have been trying to run a restaurant since high school. Elian and Lucia have always been good restaurateurs but I... not so much. No matter how hard I tried, I would get distracted, lose interest, or hire the wrong people, and the restaurant would fail.

"After Elian sold the brewery, I thought I could do it also, so I talked my father into loaning me the money to open the restaurant you critiqued. The only requirement was if I failed this time, I had to give it up for good and go into the real estate business with him. So, when you gave me the negative review, and the other customers joined you, confirming the assessment, I was angry because, at first, I thought Elian had put you up to it, then I thought my father had, then I was just angry at the circumstances.

"When I confronted you at the coffee shop, I thought I was going to uncover some conspiracy, and finding Elian there confirmed my belief. It wasn't until the family was together, and I confronted Elian that I realized I'd been wrong.

"Please, I know I don't deserve to be forgiven, but you have to understand how difficult it is to give up on a dream, even if the dream is only to outsmart your cousin."

"So..." his mother said. Ian sighed in frustration.

"So," he continued, "I'm very sorry for my actions, and Mama is right. Elian must really love you, or he'd never have stood up for you like that."

"Good boy," his mama said. "Now, go get the car started. I'll be right down."

Señora Alverez came over, put her arms around me, then kissed my cheek. "I hope to see you at one of our Sunday dinners," she said before she left.

After she was gone, Kristine came into the office and sat down. "So, what are you going to do?" she asked.

"I don't know," I said, shaking my head. "Elian put himself on the line with the people he loves the most to defend my honor, even after I refused to give him a chance. That is the opposite of Peter and his mother.

Elian stood by me and continued to do so, even after I turned into the ice queen."

Kristine giggled, "You can certainly be an ice queen. That is for *damned* sure."

I gave her a nasty look, yet she came over and hugged me. "I love Mrs. Alverez," she said. "I dream of being a mama like her one day."

"I know. Terrifying, isn't she?" I asked.

Kristine nodded. "Maybe I need to hire her to do an advice column for parents with adult children."

I could tell she was joking, but I could also see the wheels were really turning in her head.

"You really never stop, do you?"

"What?" she asked. "We are at work, I'm just doing my job. Back to Elian. It sounds like you need to have a talk with him."

I agreed. "I think I'm going to do that now," I muttered and started to walk out the door.

"I still hate you for catching the Cuban prince," she called after me.

I caught the Alverezes as they were leaving the parking garage. I waved them down and went to señora Alverez's side, and when she rolled her window down, I asked, "Where is Elian today?"

Señora Alverez squealed with delight. "He's back home at his parents' house. Get in. We'll take you with us."

The ride to their condo was uneventful, as if nothing had happened. Señora Alverez talked about everything from her niece's restaurant to the condo buildings and how Ian and his father were going to tackle some new buildings on some land north of the city.

Instead of being angry, Ian seemed to glow under his mother's pride. This was clearly the best outcome for him as well.

When we got to the building, señora Alverez made a phone call and when someone answered, she said into the phone, "Elian has a visitor." I couldn't tell what was said, but it was clear that whoever was on the other line was aware señora Alverez had come to see me.

I heard brief parts of the conversation, but eventually, señora Alverez said, "Yes, he came back with us."

Then, I heard a squeal, and señora Alverez took the phone from her ear, smiling blankly at me, pretending like nothing was going on. I knew then without asking that the person on the other end of the line was Elian's mother. Señora Alverez hung up the phone a moment later and said, "Elian will be down in a moment to get you."

It took less than a moment; one second I was talking to señora Alverez, the next Elian was standing in front of me, unshaven, hair a mess and beautiful.

"Hi... hi," he said sheepishly.

"Hi," I said and glanced around, noticing we had quite an audience of family members around the bar.

"Do you have someplace private we could talk?" I asked.

"Do you want to go down to the beach?"

I smiled. "That would be perfect.

As we walked down the stairs to the beach exit, I leaned over and kissed Elian. "I've really missed you," I said.

"I've missed you, too. I've missed you more than I've ever missed anyone," he said.

By the time we reached the beach, we were holding hands. Elian looked over at me and said, "I'm so sorry about my cousin. I'm sorry I didn't tell you…"

I stopped him. "You don't have anything to be sorry for. I overreacted. You were right not to tell me your cousin owned the restaurant. It would've been unprofessional and biased if you had. Did you know that he and your aunt were coming to see me today?"

Elian winced. "No, I didn't know, or I'd have stopped them."

"I'm glad they did. Actually, it took your aunt to get me to pull my head out of my ass and realize how much I missed and needed you."

"Really?" Elian asked in surprise.

"Yeah, really. It also helps to know your family doesn't hate me."

"No, they're all pissed at Ian. *We* are *all* pissed at Ian."

"Good, 'cause I'm still pissed at him, too, but I shouldn't punish you."

Elian came up to me, took my head in his hands, and kissed me. Then, he said, "I thought my heart was going to break in half without you." A small tear escaped down his face.

"Oh, baby," I said, emotion hitting me in the solar plexus. "I'm here, now."

We stood, kissing, hugging, and then staring out over the water. Neither of us said much more than the occasional reminder of how much we'd missed each other.

Finally, I got the courage to say what I was thinking. "I saw my ex, Peter, when I was in Austin."

Elian's light seemed to dim with that statement. He continued staring at the water. I could tell he was thinking the worst was about to happen.

"Elian, can you look at me, please?" I asked.

"Not if you are going to tell me you are getting back with your ex," he replied.

I laughed. "Fat chance of that ever happening."

Elian turned to me as some of his panic had begun to recede.

"Seeing Peter brought back some pretty nasty memories and reminded me why I'd blocked off my heart. I need to admit I was always waiting for him to come back, and that is a big reason I kept you at arms length this whole time." I sighed and returned my gaze back out toward the sea.

"When I saw him, I knew immediately I never wanted to be with him again. In fact, I tried to get him to leave, but he kept pushing. I already told you some of the circumstances. I admit, my heart assumed you would do the same. Peter wanted me to come back to him, but I explained how important it was for my partner, my spouse, to be there for me. Not that we won't ever disagree, but at least I need to know, when there is a conflict between me and my sweetheart's family, that he'd at least give me the benefit of the doubt. Peter didn't do that, and maybe I could forgive him, but I'd never forget."

"Then, my jackass cousin does the same damned thing here?"

"Yeah, he did, but you didn't do the same thing. You stood up for me because you knew I was telling the truth. That is what is different." I took Elian's face in my hands, saying, "Mi amor, you are my one, my defender. It was very brave to stand up to someone you care about even if they are wrong. When your aunt came in this morning and explained that to me, I realized I needed to see you and to thank you for being brave... for me."

"Are you still breaking up with me?" Elian asked.

"That's up to you, Elian. In the end, I'm the one who has been acting like an ass. Do you forgive me?"

Elian didn't respond but grabbed me in another huge kiss. He held onto me like he was afraid I'd disappear if he let go.

When Elian finally pulled back, he looked me in the eye and said, "I never want to lose you again. I'll gladly kick Ian's ass again if you want me to."

I laughed. "I think you just *want* to kick Ian's ass but that isn't necessary. He apologized, and I could tell he was sincere. Besides, both you and his mom have sort of already handed him his ass on a platter. I think we can let him off the hook now."

"If you say so," Elian replied, then kissed me again. "Wanna go play in the ocean?"

"I don't have a bathing suit," I replied.

"I do. Come on up. We'll get changed, then go play. Can you surf?"

"Hell, no," I said. "I grew up inland. I never had a chance to try."

"Then today is your lucky day," Elian teased, pulling me up with him.

We spent the day playing in the waves, then went to Lucia's restaurant for dinner. When we finished eating, we sat on the beach, the sunset behind us as we watched the sky pinken above the ocean.

"I think I'm in love with you, Martin. Is that okay with you?"

I chuckled. "I *know* I'm in love with you, so that is perfect with me."

Elian leaned up on his elbow. "Really, you *are* in love with me?"

"Hook, line, and sinker," I replied. "I think that is the main reason I reacted like I did when your cousin went apeshit on me. I assumed I'd lose you, and it really knocked my life into a tailspin. But, Elian, I didn't give you a chance to be you. It wasn't fair."

Elian continued to gaze at me. "I'll never intentionally hurt you like that," he said. "As long as you give me a chance, I promise to do my best to do what is right by you."

"Then," I replied, "I promise to always give you a chance. Even if I'm terrified."

Elian rolled on top of me and kissed me. I could feel his erection under his swimsuit. He ground it into me and whispered, "Now, let's go find somewhere where I can make love to you. I want to fuck you in every way possible to make up for the past two weeks." Elian wiggled his eyebrows at me and said, "Two weeks is a long time to come up with the different moves I plan to use on you."

I laughed. "Want to come back to my place?"

"No need. I bought a condo here and closed on it last week. I already have a bed in it."

"Really?" I smiled. "Then, by all means, let's go christen your new condo!"

Elian pulled me up, and we all but ran to his new front door.

***

Continue reading for an excerpt from
Another Chance With Love

ANOTHER CHANCE WITH LOVE

Chance Series:

Book Two

Blake Allwood

Trevor

I got out and walked directly to the lake and sat on the same bench I'd sat on with Grandpa last time I was here. Luckily no one was out and about yet except a few kids on the playground, so I had enough space to have the talk I really wanted to have.

"Grandpa," I said quietly, hoping no one could hear me, "I need some guidance. As you probably know, I now have a baby of my own, and although Aunt Doris is helping out, I worry that I'm not going to be enough. That I don't have what it takes to be a good dad. I keep having the same nightmare over and over that I somehow broke his arm. Like dad did to me."

It was the first time I'd admitted that out loud, and the emotions around that dream crept up on me with a vengeance. Before I could stop myself, I was crying, and I was not shedding delicate tears. No, I was crying like a crazy person.

Before I knew it, a hand rested on my shoulder. My first thought was Grandpa. But when I looked up and saw Peter's face, I was full-out mortified.

"Fuck," I said out loud, quickly wiping at my tears. "I thought I was alone."

"You were. Sorry, I drive through the park to get to work. When I saw you get out of your car, I followed you."

"Well, shit. Now you think I'm insane?"

"No, I don't. I know you have to be under intense pressure raising Luka on your own." Peter sat next to me, then put his arm around me and pulled me to his chest. Damn, if that wasn't the worst thing he could've done. I came here to have a pity fest, and I sure didn't need anyone to witness it. But the stress of raising Luka, learning to be a dad, and now, fuck, Peter... Peter was part of the stress. Thinking about dating again was what pushed me over the edge.

Instead of pulling away from Peter, like any sane person would, I let him hold me while my tears flowed. Luckily, I wasn't one to linger on my emotions for long, and so after I got my cryfest done and over with, I pulled back. "I'm so sorry, Peter. You caught me at a really bad time. I should be getting back."

"Wait, I'm the one who should be sorry for getting in the way of a moment to yourself, but when I saw you were upset, I couldn't help it. It seemed like you might need someone by your side."

I wiped the tears, then let my head fall back on the bench. "Peter, I'm in no shape to be dating anyone right now. When my aunt told me you and Leonardo were coming for dinner tonight, I sort of flipped. On the one hand, I rushed to the store to buy ingredients for dinner, and on the other, I'm an emotional train wreck."

I looked around at the lake and the trail that worked its way around it. "This is the last place I sat with my grandpa before he died. He's the one I could talk to about anything. Sex, friendships, I even had a long conversation with him once about whether or not I should use drugs when a friend in middle school was trying to get me to try them. When Luka's mom left him with me, I was shocked and scared shitless, but I knew as long as I had Aunt Doris, I'd be fine... we'd be fine. When I went on that trip with your mom, I didn't worry about him one bit, knowing my aunt would keep him safe. Now, she's met someone and is so giddy over him. I've never seen her that way, and all I can think about is she's going to end up moving to Europe, and what the hell am I going to do then? I know, I know, it's selfish and cruel of me to wish Leonardo never showed up, but the fear is there, nonetheless. Then this morning, she told me you were going to come over, and I could tell this was a set-up and, Peter, even if you are interested in me, which you probably aren't, but even if you were, I can't date someone. I have a baby. I just graduated from college, and I couldn't even find the time to walk across the damned stage. There's no way I can date someone, be a new parent, and continue to function like a normal human being."

Peter listened to me rant, and even though the embarrassment grew as the words spewed from my mouth, I wasn't capable of stopping them.

Finally, Peter leaned back, keeping his arm around me. "If you're so worried about dating, then let's not date. Let's just hang out together. No strings, no commitments, just two guys hanging out." He stared at me with a look of concern on his face. "I'm sorry I put pressure on you. I didn't mean to, but I do like you, I liked you from the minute I met you even if I did want to tar and feather you for interfering with my life. But in the short time I've known you, everything has turned into something good. First, you got my mother to apologize to Martin, and Martin actually forgave her. I don't even have words for how important that was or how that healed all three of us. Then your home was exactly what my client needed, and we're building his shops around its architecture. And you, I don't want to put any more pressure on you but, to be honest, you are the first guy I've met since Martin left that I want to get to know better. That means something to me. I wondered if I'd ever date again and now, I can see that it's possible. So even if you aren't interested in dating me, I want to get to know you better. I want to get to know Luka better, too. It'd be fun for me to spend some time with a baby. So, if you're willing, let's try that, OK?"

Peter's look was hopeful, almost childlike, and I smiled. "I don't understand what a handsome man like you sees in a sleep-deprived single dad, but sure,

I'd like to have someone to hang out with, too. Maybe the friend thing might work."

Peter's smile grew mischievous. "Can I be a friend that kisses you?"

I gazed at him, then down at his very luscious lips, and before I could stop myself, I leaned into him, taking his mouth with my own. All the concern and frustration bubbled into that kiss as I pulled his head closer. My tongue tangled with his, and the heat magnified instantly. Luckily, he pulled back and sighed. "Let's do this again when you aren't feeling so vulnerable." Then he looked around and said, "If that gets any deeper, we're going to turn Springvale Park into a porn scene."

I knew I was blushing. One minute I was saying, "Let's be friends," and the next I almost humped him in the park.

"You'd be wise just to run away and never see me again," I whined.

"Um, after that kiss, you can bet that's *not* gonna happen. I'm going to be like a lost puppy now following you around, begging for another kiss like that one."

I chuckled. "You can't say you weren't warned."

Peter smiled and pulled me up with him. "I need to get to work. Richmond has my day filled from now" – he looked at his watch – "until tonight."

"I need to get back, too. I'm sure Aunt Doris is going to be ready for a break by the time I get home."

Peter kissed my forehead, peered into my eyes, and just as it appeared he was about to come in for round two, he pulled me into a hug. "I'll see you tonight," he said and turned to leave.

He turned around again and smiled that million-dollar smile at me, and it took all I had to keep my knees from melting under me. "I'm so screwed," I said out loud. Then he turned away and jogged toward the parking lot. "So fucking screwed," I said again as I shook my head.

***

Purchase ***Another Chance With Love*** now at:

blakeallwood.com/booklink/2047692